KINGS OF CHAOS

Crossroads

KENTUCKY

Charles Kelley

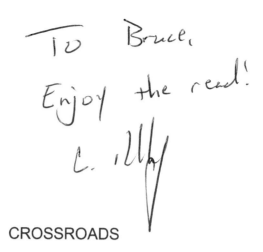

To Bruce,

Enjoy the read!

C. Illy

CROSSROADS

Book 1 in the Kings of Chaos Motorcycle Club series

By Charles Kelley

Kings of Chaos Motorcycle Club logo designed by Steven Hayslett

Cover design by CK2 Imaging

For my ol' lady, Chrissy, who'll ride with me through good weather and bad;

the driving force in my life.

ACKNOWLEDGMENTS

Huge thanks to Adam K. Moore. Without your encouragement, motivation, and creativity, this book may never have been completed. Your eagle-eye for editing has made this story as tolerable as it is.

Let me offer an equal amount of praise and appreciation to Christian Scully. Your positive response and feedback helped get this manuscript to the printer. You both are responsible for making this story everything it is, so I blame you two for everything that's wrong with it.

I simply cannot recommend their works enough. The ongoing series, Compendium Twenty-Three by Adam K. Moore is one of the most original stories I've ever read, and the ongoing series, The Chronicles of Erika Lorenz by Christian Scully gives an all-new, fresh twist to vampire lore.

Chapter 1

Imagine if you were in a situation where you turned your back on everything you held dear. You spend years of your life chasing something you've always wanted. You get close to guys that have no fear. You earn their trust and they let you into their inner circle. Then one day, you're faced with the toughest choice of your life, and you decide that what you've worked so hard for and yearned for isn't really what you thought you wanted. Unfortunately, I don't have to imagine that situation. I'm living it. And things are about to get a little hairy. Let me put it this way; you never want to double cross an outlaw motorcycle club if you have plans to make it to your next birthday.

You might think being pinned down by gunfire behind a dumpster isn't the most ideal time to analyze past mistakes and bad life choices. On the contrary though, I'm not sure there is a much better time at all. It's not like you can go anywhere. Your bike is lying in a heap on the ground about fifteen feet away thanks to the surprise ambush you rolled into on your way to the clubhouse that morning. If you peek out from behind your cover, then you're tempting your own fate by catching the business end of a bullet. It's natural to think back about where you went wrong and all of the poor decisions you made to land you in such a tough spot. Thoughts about how your life could be so much different if you made just one decision differently. Nevermind the difference if you changed all of your previous choices that got you here. What? That's not a scenario you can relate to? Must just be me then.

"Better get comfortable back there, you prick!" came a grizzled shout from inside the clubhouse, followed by a potshot meant to keep my attention and remind me that there was no turning back.

Maybe I should start from the beginning. My name is Will. I grew up with motor oil in my blood. My entire life has been spent in the seat of a motorcycle. My dad owned one vehicle for as long as I can remember – a 1948 Harley-Davidson Panhead. I was raised on the back of that Harley, and I thought I was untouchable. On the days dad was sober enough to drop me off at school, I would see all the other kids' eyes get wide and they'd start whispering to each other as we pulled up to the curb at the bus drop-off zone. I would hop off, and stroll past all of them with my shades still on and my head held high. I was a badass…even in fifth grade. My dad would twist the throttle a couple times before releasing the clutch and rolling away, his Kings of Chaos patch showing with pride on the back of his jacket. It was his way of saying "See you later," as well as his way of irritating the institution.

On days when dad had "important business" to take care of (or was too inebriated to drive) my grandpa would be waiting to pick me up outside of the school. He would weave his way through the idling school busses and park front and center on the sidewalk. Of course, this drove the teachers crazy because it was a safety hazard for the other students, but have you ever tried to tell a biker what to do? Of course you haven't…nobody does.

So grandpa would roll up, drop his kick stand and lean back on his massive 1945 1,200cc Indian Chief. He never liked to talk about being in World War II, but he went on and on about the thrill of riding the military issued Indians overseas. To help with getting reacquainted with civilian life, the first thing my grandfather did when he returned from abroad was go straight from the boat to a dealership and buy an Indian motorcycle. He kept the machine clean, but you could easily tell that it was ridden regularly. Like he always said, "A clean bike is a sure sign you're talking to a biker. A sparkling bike is a sure sign that you're not."

So you see, my family was raised in the biker boom in the mid-twentieth century. My grandpa came home from the war looking for something to give him a similar rush that he experienced overseas. That rush was found in the saddle of a motorcycle. With his pension from the military and a modest lifestyle learned from The Great Depression, he was able to spend all of his time in the wind, so to speak. Grandpa lived as a free spirit – he made sure that my dad was taken care of, usually at grandma's expense, but then he lived his life the way he wanted to. He loved his family, and loved the quiet, alone time he was granted on his motorcycle almost just as much.

My dad, Lee, never served in the military but he grew up admiring grandpa's freedom. Needless to say, dad wanted the same lifestyle with none of the work. He loved it almost to the same degree as grandpa, but liked a little more camaraderie between rides, which led him to spending a lot of his time standing still at a local biker bar.

After awhile of earning his reputation as a legit, badass biker, dad was approached by a member of the Kings of Chaos – the local motorcycle club that was known in the area for being loud, rowdy, rude, and generally unruly, inquiring if he would like to start the process of becoming a member of the club. We lived in a small rural town, so the club was well-known among the locals and law enforcement alike. The undesirable behavior from the club was typically overlooked since they provided a sense of "protection" for the neighborhood. Truth be told, most of the protection they offered came in the form of extortion of business owners. The club would approach a proprietor and offer to make sure their business was looked after. What they meant to say was, "Give us some money every month, or your place might get banged up a little bit." However, the club was very protective of its turf, so if there was ever any fuss from outsiders, the club was always there to take care of their town.

With dad's attitude toward the lifestyle and craving the recognition the club would provide, he took no time to agree to become a "hang around" with the Kings.

Being a hang around is the first step of the initiation process to become a full patch member. Hang arounds are required to be at every club function, but are not technically members in the sense that they wear no patches with the club's logo and they're usually not even permitted to attend official club meetings, often referred to as church. Essentially, as a hang around, dad was simply getting to know the members and earn their trust. Since that was basically how he earned the opportunity to be an official hang around though, that period didn't last long. Within a matter of weeks, dad's trust and level of commitment were clear and unquestioned.

In an uncharacteristically quick decision for a motorcycle club, they gave dad his prospect patch after only 3 weeks as a hang around. This was the next step in the initiation process, and along with it came the first of three patches, known as colors, for the back of his leather jacket, or cut. This phase required even more loyalty and servitude. At this point, my dad basically became the club's servant and had to submit to anything any member of the club wanted at anytime. If the club wanted to go for a long ride but didn't want the hassle of worrying about breaking down and being stranded on the side of the road, then dad was forced to leave his bike behind and follow the pack in a pick-up truck and trailer. If the Kings threw a party and their clubhouse got trashed, then it was up to dad to be the first one in the next morning to get it all cleaned up…only after he stayed outside for the entire party acting as security. And he still wasn't allowed to attend church or generally have a voice on club matters.

That was all way before I was born. By the time I entered the picture, dad was a full-patch member. That meant that the back of his leather jacket featured 3 patches – the top rocker that displayed the name of the club, the large middle patch that showed the skull wearing a V-Twin crown logo of the MC (motorcycle club), and the bottom rocker that stated the location of the club or that particular chapter. There was also a fourth, small, unofficial patch that was worn with just as much pride. It consisted of the outline of a diamond shape that simply stated "1%er."

That little patch along the side of the club's colors demanded attention. Its significance was garnered following the Hollister, California riot in 1947. The American Motorcycle Association released a statement following that incident claiming that 99% of motorcycle riders are good, upstanding, law-abiding citizens… implying that the other 1% were outlaws. Those who were deemed to be part of the 1% embraced the saying whole-heartedly. Essentially, that diamond-shaped patch loudly screams to everyone in the vicinity to show the utmost respect or leave the club completely alone altogether.

As you can imagine, being a member of an outlaw motorcycle club includes doing things that most people would shy away from. Those things could include busting up a shop in order to extort money from the owner, transport and/or sell drugs, guns or other ill-gotten merch, assault somebody for any given reason, or even worse – like shoot at former club members that piss them off. (Sorry, that's not something that's easy to forget and move on from.)

That's just an example to give you a small idea of what a day of the club's "business" might include. It's not all bad though; a day in the life could just as easily be spent in the clubhouse having drinks together and sharing and reliving stories from the past. Sometimes business is even good - several times per year, the club will organize fundraisers for local charities and children's organizations. They have helped clean up debris and fallen branches after severe thunderstorms, repair damage to the local VFW building, and scrub graffiti off the face of their town's small library. In a weird sense, they really do care about the community and are mostly embraced by its citizens.

The club was good at conducting most of their business on the outskirts of city limits or at least in the dark shadows of an alley. The more attention they brought on themselves, then the more heat they had to deal with from negative publicity and worse – local law enforcement. They stayed out of the limelight for the most part, which in turn kept them out of jail.

"Hey asshole! You've made your dad reeeeeal proud!" came another shout from the clubhouse, each word dripping with sarcasm. Just to confirm my suspicion that nobody was proud of me, a bullet whizzed by my head and hit the gas tank of my bike. Fortunately, I had at least a little luck on my side as my bike didn't immediately burst into a giant fireball. "Why don't you step on out here and get dead real quick?"

"Hey! Take it easy on my bike! What did it ever do to you??" I yelled back. They don't own sarcasm, and I opt to use that as my number one defense mechanism.

So where was I? Oh right, my family and the club. By the time I was old enough to start piecing things together, dad had grown distant from me and our family. The questions that I badgered him with incessantly might have had something to do with that. That left me to basically fend for myself. Mom had split long ago, and by the time I was old enough to take care of my basic needs, dad decided he was done doing it for me and left it up to my grandparents to look after me. But even that was done from a distance.

Don't get me wrong, it's not like I was abandoned and left to survive on my own. Dad just left my life up to me. I knew how to clean, dress and feed myself. I also knew what hurt, what was dangerous, and how to avoid those things. Assuming that I had a little common sense, dad didn't see the need to interfere with nature…I could figure the rest out on my own. Even when dad was around physically, his mental state was a completely different story. There were two typical scenarios whenever I got to spend time around him. Either he was completely distracted from working on his bike, or he was beyond too-drunk-to-care what was going on around him. The former of those situations was my favorite, because it offered about the only time that I ever got to see my dad as a mentor of sorts. As long as I stayed back and didn't block the light, then he would let me watch and try to teach me everything he could about working on the mechanics of a motorcycle. Naturally that helped fuel my interest in the subject.

By the time I was tall enough to sit in a saddle and have my feet touch the ground, I started learning how to ride. "The faster you go, the more stable the bike is," was the best (and worst) piece of advice my dad ever told me. "At slow speeds, you have to pay more attention to your balance so you don't drop the bike. Once you get going, everything evens out and the bike rides smoother," he advised. "Think of it as a spinning top; the more speed it has, the more upright it sits. Once it starts slowing down, then it starts wobbling until it eventually tips over onto its side…that's bad – don't do that."

Also at that time, dad was a lot less worried about hiding his activities from me. On any given night he would bring home any one (or more) of a handful of girls that were passed around between club members. The girls liked riding and partying with the club, so they accepted their unofficial position. I also started noticing that beer and whiskey began having company on our coffee table with marijuana and cocaine. Dad also seemed to have a lot more money than we were accustomed too, and with that came the addition of a gun or two…or seven.

Chapter 2

Fast forward a bit to my teenage years. Somehow, I managed to escape my pre-determined destiny of hooligan, degenerate biker. I ended up leaving the area that I was born and raised, and the only place that I ever spent any time of my life in. The prospect of moving on to something completely new to me was a little scary, but in the back of my mind I knew that staying where I was would be even scarier…it was only a matter of time. I left our small town in the lonely hills of Rough River Falls, Kentucky for much greener pastures in the United States Air Force.

The further I got away from my roots, the clearer my head became. I started seeing an accurate portrait of my family for the first time. I saw how other people were raised in stable households with parents that actually paid attention and cared about their children. The longer I stayed gone, the more resentment grew in the pit of my stomach. Not resentment toward my father or grandparents, I think they did the best they could with what they knew. Dad was raised in a home with a loving mother and a father who didn't realize how detrimental his absence – both physical and mental – was. That upbringing created my dad who turned to motorcycles and the MC to serve as his extended family because that's what he knew. He wasn't raised in a typical household, so he didn't know how to create one for me. No, it was my resentment for the club life that grew stronger by the day.

Without the Kings's influence, maybe my dad could've figured out how to be a real-life parent. Maybe my mom wouldn't have left. And maybe, just maybe, I could've played little league baseball with friends from school, or even just had friends from school. You can probably imagine how few parents are willing to allow their offspring to hang out at a druggie, biker's house. Thanks for helping me fit in, dad. That's where my stellar personality and people skills stem from.

Seeing the importance of structure and order, I ultimately turned to a career in security forces while in the Air Force. For multiple reasons, it was a match made in heaven. It helped me escape the deviant lifestyle that I was raised in. On top of that, I had a chance to make a difference for others who were in similar situations to what I went through. I could relate to them and I knew what they were going through, so I knew how to help them. Further still, it gave me the adrenaline high that I had gotten so used to from riding.

"Miller!" I barked in a whisper. "On 3...2...1...GO!" On my mark, my patrol partner stepped from the side of the door frame we were flanking and kicked it in with authority. I charged in, weapon drawn. "HALT! DON'T MOVE!" I commanded to the lone airman, sitting on the couch in his on-base apartment. He was caught totally off-guard, but displayed no signs of surprise. I think I saw a flash of awe in his eyes from the total bad-ass moment Miller and I just had, busting through his door. Or maybe I just saw that because that's what I wanted to see. No way to tell for sure.

Our bust went smoothly. The suspect never gave us any trouble, already knowing he didn't stand a chance of talking his way out of the current predicament. He was on property owned by the federal government with pot plants stashed in his linen closet. What an idiot.

"Did you see the look on his face when we broke through the door, gangbusters style? I was waiting for him to make a move; make a run for it or at least try lying his way out of it...*some*thing," Miller said, taking a sip from his coffee cup. "But once I saw the look on his face, I thought the most he might do was shit his pants!" he spat out before laughter took over and he couldn't say anything else.

I let out a chuckle before I took a drink of sweet tea. Miller and I usually hit up the same little diner outside of the confines of Lackland Air Force Base in San Antonio, Texas after work to wind down from our shift, and tonight was no different. Our waitress brought our regular orders of BBQ brisket sandwiches, mashed potatoes and gravy, and sweet corn. "Man, Miller, we've been on a helluva roll lately, huh?" I asked. Without waiting for his response, I continued, "tonight's bust, the car that was riding dirty through the East Gate last week with all those pills, The airman we caught selling guns to unauthorized civilians a couple weeks before that, and those two civilian BX employees we chased across base for stealing from the Base Exchange before that. I don't know if all this shit is normal or it's just us being good at what we do, but it's been nuts lately. Sarge called me in to talk to me about everything a few days ago. Asked how me and you keep ending up in the middle of everything. Has he said anything to you?"

"Actually, he caught me in the locker room the other day after PT. Basically asked me the same stuff and wondered how I liked working with you. Come to think of it, most of his questions were about you. Who took the lead on most of our stops; who called the shots on our busts; if I felt comfortable taking your orders; or if I ever felt in danger from your decisions. I didn't think much of it at the time with the way he sprinkled other conversation in, but now that I think about it it was a pretty pointed conversation," Miller concluded.

I hadn't given it a thought before then, but after hearing Miller my mind kicked into overdrive. Was I overstepping my boundaries as a Senior Airmen; upsetting my superiors? I've always followed the chain of command – when I got information about the airman cultivating pot plants in his barracks, I went straight to my Staff Sergeant. I never asked Miller to do something I wouldn't be willing to do myself, and I don't think I've ever held my rank over his head, since he's a pay-grade below me. I've always tried to exemplify the standards and expectations of my superiors, which has up until now always garnered respect from them. Now it seems I may have brought some unwanted scrutiny my way.

After we picked our plates clean and finished winding down from the adrenaline pump from our bust, we called it a night.

Another couple months passed without anything particularly noteworthy happening. The end of my 6 year commitment was approaching fast, and I planned on separating from the Air Force to see what kind of job I could find at a civilian police department. I appreciated everything the Air Force had provided for me, but I didn't care much for the idea of having to relocate and not having much input as to where.

"McGee," barked my Senior NCO from his desk as I walked by his office. "A word?"

"Yes, Senior?" I asked as I entered his office. My casual response came from the familiarity of a good working relationship, but I still stood at parade rest out of respect while he addressed me.

"I heard you started the separation paperwork. What are your plans after this?" he inquired. I filled him in on my intentions of looking into the public sector of law enforcement. "I'm sure you've heard that people have been asking about you lately," he continued. I nodded along. "When you began the separation process, the DEA started looking into you. They were aware of your work and were hoping to get their claws into you as soon as they could. Anyway, they came calling; asking me about your abilities, work ethic, strengths, weaknesses, leadership – all that crap." Suddenly, the conversation I had with Miller several months ago was starting to add up. "I was asked to give you this business card when the time came. They are expecting your call once your service ends."

"Thank you, Senior," I said as I spun on my heels and marched out of his office.

Luckily, my last couple of weeks on active duty went by relatively quickly with no real action. Admittedly, my mind had been wandering.

Chapter 3

"Listen Will, I don't want to beat around the bush," came the voice from the other end of the phone. As usual, I had followed orders and put in a call to the DEA agent that my sergeant had given me the card for. The beginning of the conversation had been slightly frustrating until this point, with me being questioned about loyalties to people from my past and my opinions of my hometown and the locals - meaning the Kings. The agent had to be careful to test my allegiances, but not give away any sensitive information in case I couldn't be trusted. Finally, I had thoroughly convinced him that I was not particularly fond of the club or their activities and was on board with whatever he had left to discuss. "I'm not sure how connected you've kept with things in Kentucky since you've left, but I have no doubt you've heard about the mishap with Representative Olsen's son overdosing on cocaine. Due to the high profile nature of the case, we've felt a lot of pressure to make a bust, but it's not like we can just walk into town and start arresting people. I think we all know where the cocaine came from, but we have no way of getting the information we need."

"Which is where I come in," I finished his thought for him. "With my history and past connections, you think I can get into the club quickly and without suspicion. I probably can – no problem there. But how do you suggest I get my information to you?"

"That's the tricky part," was his reply.

Yeah, no shit.

"Since it's such a small town and everybody knows everybody, it's not like we could just assign a support team to move in without throwing up some serious red flags for any locals who might be paying attention. We kind of hit the jackpot with your separation from the Air Force and your desire to live somewhere familiar. My proposal is once we get you processed in to the agency and placed back in Rough River Falls, then you will act as your own unit. You won't have any handlers. You also won't have any backup. You'll be on your own on this. You will collect all the intel you can and send updates at regular intervals. Once you have everything tied up in a neat little bow, then you'll get the hell outta Dodge and we'll send in a team to handle all the dirty work."

I liked the idea of having control over where I'd be working. I'd be on my own for fear that having a handler nearby would result in my cover getting blown and probably getting both of us killed. I was required to send status reports which had its own set of problems – I couldn't have the postmaster making comments about me sending mail to the DEA. In small town Kentucky that would be something worth talking about, and I don't need my business being leaked through the local gossip channels. I also couldn't sneak off on a regular basis without some sort of plausible excuse in case anybody got curious, so I ended up dropping packages at various places around town at all times of day and night in order for unknown travelers to gather on their way innocently through town.

All in all, it wasn't a bad gig. I was able to live some place familiar, which was nice, and I also got to focus on taking down the organization that derailed my family.

Chapter 4

"Will McGee?? Holy shit, man! Is that you? I think I just saw a ghost! Where have you been these last few years?" came a grizzled voice from behind me.

That was the first thing I heard as I stepped into my hometown's Gas N' Go. I turned my head and shifted my eyes around to see who was addressing me while I topped off the fountain drink that I was currently pouring. Once I sucked down a little of the foam off the top and popped a lid on the cup, I spun around and saw a behemoth standing a couple of feet away. The gravelly voice fit the physical description of this guy perfectly.

In front of me was a bear of a man standing 6'4" tall and weighing in around 275 pounds, with a full grown beard that a mountain man would be proud of. Not that his beard would be outdone, there was just as much arm hair and back hair sprouting out of the openings of his leather vest. "Good Lord, Griz, you're uglier than ever," I responded without having to look at the name patch on the front of his vest. He gave me a hard stare, not sure what to think or do before the tough façade broke and his face brightened with a big smile and he gave me a warm hug.

Griz, short for Grizzly, is a patch member of the Kings and I've known him my whole life. He was given the nickname by the club due to his size and overall appearance resembling a grizzly bear. Picture a prototypical biker and there's your mental image of Griz – beer belly hanging over his belt, open leather vest with no t-shirt (but enough hair to resemble a sweater), tattoo covered arms, blue jeans, boots, fingerless leather gloves, and a thick brown beard down to his collarbone. He was always involved with whatever my dad got into.

"How the Hell have you been, man? I haven't seen you since your old man passed," Griz asked delicately.

My dad died a couple years back from liver failure. Did I not mention that earlier? Sorry, I guess it's just not something that seems like that big of a deal to be honest with you. What else can you expect when you dump alcohol and chemicals into your body like it's going out of style? Not that I wasn't sad when it happened, but we were never that close to begin with so the mourning phase was rather short-lived. That mentality toward my father probably plays a large role in my disdain for the club.

"I've been okay. Ya know, surviving. Just finished up my time in the Air Force and decided it was time to come home. I guess I just wasn't meant to wander too far," I answered.

"Air Force, huh? Your dad had mentioned you were serving but he never had many details. You could tell he was proud of you though. What did you end up getting into?"

Without giving away anything specific, I kept my answer short and sweet. I couldn't lie to the guy because he'd spot it from a mile away, plus that would just be one more thing that I would have to remember later on. "They just had me guard stuff. Did my six years and decided to call it a day. Didn't want to end up on some other continent, and kinda heard this place calling me back, so here I am."

"You should swing by the clubhouse. The guys would be excited to see you. What are you riding these days?" Griz inquired.

"To be honest with you, I haven't ridden for quite awhile. I sold my bike after dad died. It seemed like a bitter reminder that I didn't want to live with, ya know? The old man did leave me his Panhead though. It's just been sitting in storage since he passed, but it might be about time to dust it off. Could be a nice tribute to him to clean it up and get it running again…probably wouldn't take much either. Fresh gas and new tires should just about do it with the way he always kept it. Worst case scenario, I might have to rebuild the carburetors if there's any gummed up gas that's been sitting in them but it shouldn't be any worse than that I wouldn't imagine."

"Bring it by the shop. I'll clear off a lift you can use. You'll have free run of the place – whatever tools you need, just pick up the tab for any parts. Between us and the club, we should have that thing breathing fire in no time."

"Sounds good, Griz," I replied. "Just do me a favor…don't tell anybody I'm around yet. Let it be a surprise when I show up with the old man's bike, huh?" And just like that, I had my foot in the door.

I turned toward the cashier to pay for my fountain drink while Griz waited patiently to pay for his gas. Unfortunately, the next guy that walked into the small convenience store wasn't as patient. We hadn't noticed the BMW that had been sitting by the lone working gas pump during our brief little catch-up until the driver stepped through the door. He looked at the two of us with an irritated glare and looked down to his shiny watch. You could tell he wasn't a local with his luxury sedan, fancy watch, and nice clothes. His hair had gel in it, if that tells you anything – Rough River Falls, Kentucky isn't a place for guys with hair gel. Once Griz stepped up to the counter, the guy made some snarky comment about the gas pump not being a parking spot as he shoved through the door on his way back outside. Big mistake.

Griz peeled away from the counter and followed the yuppie outside toward the gas pump. The out-of-towner wasn't aware that he was being stalked, and as he rounded the hood of his car to get in and wait for Griz to leave so he could pull up next to the pump, a giant callused hand grabbed the back of his neck and "encouraged" him along. Griz yanked the car door open and threw the stranger into the driver's seat, all while explaining that patience is a virtue. At the end of the exchange, Griz smacked the guy's cheek. Hard. You could tell the visitor didn't know what to say, do, or think. He just sat in his car with a shocked look of disbelief on his ever-reddening face. For all I could tell, he might've peed a little bit.

As Griz mounted his Harley at an intentionally slow pace, glowering at his new friend, the guy took his first notice of the Kings of Chaos Skull King patch emblazoned across the gargantuan leather vest. I could see the realization in the guy's face, and I think he knew how incredibly dumb, and lucky, he just was. I just shook my head as I climbed into my truck.

*****

A couple days passed before I finally decided that I needed to leave my apartment and get some fresh air. Now that I was back home, I wasn't nearly as excited to be there as I thought I would be. Regardless, I was on the job and couldn't just sit in my living room all day. I didn't want to rush over to the Kings' clubhouse and seem too eager and pathetic to establish a connection with them but I didn't want to wait too long either, in case Griz couldn't keep our secret.

On the way to my truck, I glanced in the open door of the apartment next to mine. There was a small, disheveled child running around in nothing but a diaper, his greasy hair matted to his head, and dirt smudges all over his face, arms, and chest. The next thing I noticed was the strung out woman passed out on the couch with her half-burnt cigarette dangling from her snoring mouth. I stopped for a split second until a scrawny male threw the storm door open and walked right past me on his way to the piece of crap motorcycle parked in front of the building…his Kings of Chaos patch staring right back at me, taunting me. The scumbag hopped on his hog, fired it up and rode away without a second thought about the little boy or his fire hazard of a mom. My disdain for the Kings multiplied tenfold in those few seconds. My family had been broken due to the club, and seeing it happen all over again to another helpless child was all I could take.

As I pulled into the parking lot for Griz's Garage (you bet that's the name of the place, and why wouldn't it be?!) I received several curious stares. Some were faces I'd never seen before, but then there were the regulars I was looking for standing inside an empty garage bay. They all had on the familiar black vests with the black and blue Kings of Chaos patches. As I pulled up in an unfamiliar truck, the old-timers barely paid any attention to my presence, until my truck swung around and they caught a glimpse of the precious cargo on my flatbed trailer. The recognition registered on their faces the second they saw dad's Harley Davidson – before any of them even recognized me personally.

They started approaching the truck as I slid out from the driver's seat when the leader of the older trio slowed his pace and took a step back, squinting his eyes behind his sunglasses. "Will??" came the question in complete disbelief. Apparently, Griz hadn't let our surprise slip and didn't say anything as this little scene played out either.

"What's it take to get a little help around this shit-hole?" I asked half-jokingly. I started cracking my knuckles to calm my nerves. I could tell that my identity still hadn't been completely recognized. "Hey RJ, Griz told me to swing by and get some help getting this old junker running again," I said thumbing toward the classic bike that would hardly be considered a junker in any sense of the word.

The instant I said his name, his face softened and his approach quickened. (Outsiders don't call bikers by their road name.) He met me, along with Griz and one other member, with a big hug and then started in with the small talk. In a matter of minutes we were all caught up and they had made their way to my trailer. "Prospect!" RJ beckoned. "Get this bike unloaded…and you better not scratch it!"

RJ serves as the club's Vice President. He's an original member, and his founding father status is highly regarded through the ranks of the club. He took the VP position when the club's second President was elected. RJ had no desire to run the club, but his wisdom and experience made him a perfect mentor for a slightly younger, first-time President. As the VP, he can keep the club from getting too side-tracked at times, but doesn't have the headache of having to make all the calls.

To his right is a shorter guy everyone calls El C. Short for El Capitán, this is the guy who's in charge of organizing club events such as charity rides. Appropriately, his nickname is derived from his status in the club as Road Captain. He is responsible for communicating with everyone behind him in the pack. Using hand signals, it's up to him to warn other riders of hazards in the road, sudden stops, and if there are any cops lurking ahead. Because of these duties, the only people who ride in front of El C in formation are the Prez and Vice Prez. El C has been around long enough to know my old man, and his bike, but not long enough for me to be too familiar with him. He patched in maybe a year or two before I joined the Air Force.

As I was getting a little more acquainted with El C, the prospect that RJ had yelled for had jogged over and hopped up on my trailer. He had his back to me, kneeling down to unfasten the tie-down straps that were securing the motorcycle in place. Once he stepped around to the other side of the bike to roll it off the trailer, I couldn't help but recognize a familiar face from high school. I decided to keep my focus with RJ, Griz, and El C for the time being so they wouldn't feel disrespected by me acknowledging the prospect in the middle of our conversation. The hierarchy in a motorcycle club is very rigid, and respect is the number one priority during any interaction with a club member. Write that down – you never want to disrespect an MC or member in any way…it's an especially bad idea to approach them with a hidden agenda, but we'll get back to that soon enough.

Through our conversation, I picked up on a little more information about the club's current structure, but it's not like the guys were blurting out everything I wanted to know. Club business is for club members. Period. Honestly, they were probably sharing more with me than they should have been just because of my historical connection. I was able to glean the other sitting officers, and how big the club had grown – that second bit of information is something that is NEVER given out…club's always keep their numbers confidential so rivals don't know who or how many people to expect if something goes down. Officers usually aren't given out either, but all you have to do is look at a few vests to see what their patches say…it's not like it's confidential intel.

To no surprise, I learned that RJ is still serving under the same Prez: Riot. That is pretty standard business. It's typical when a new Prez is elected then there is usually a whole new regime change. The sitting Prez wants to be sure to surround himself with people that he knows, feels comfortable with, and trusts completely. When I saw the VP patch on RJ's vest, I didn't have to wait to hear who the Prez was because I already knew.

Other than Griz, I learned that there was one other "official" enforcer: Mack – the Sergeant at Arms. When Riot took over, Mack would have been the natural choice for VP, but he lacks the organizational and general leadership skills required to be second in command. I've known him just as long as I've known Riot, since they both prospected at the same time when my dad was still around. My familiarity with them is somewhat limited though due to my absence. What I do know is that Mack will never go against Riot and will support him through anything. Mack also serves as Riot's unofficial confidant, so I'm sure he knows more about the club than he'll ever tell anybody. If I'm smart and careful enough, that could come in very handy.

Something that caught me a little by surprise was how much expansion Riot had focused on lately. It doesn't seem anybody knows his motive, but over the last couple of years he has introduced and approved more members than normal, and some of the old-timers haven't been too thrilled about it. I guess he's taken in some guys that don't really fit in, with his focus on quantity over quality. Not that the club is massive by any means, but compared to the original six, the current roster seems like quite a lot in such a small town.

Chapter 5

I had spent a few nights tooling on dad's old Harley and was about ready to reassemble everything that I'd had to tear apart. Several of the Kings had stopped by and offered a helping hand since I had shown up, but Riot had been noticeably absent. Since my arrival, I'm not sure the sitting Prez had even made eye contact with me. He wasn't putting out a very welcoming vibe, so I'm sure he wasn't thrilled about the other members hanging around and visiting with me...none of which stuck around more than Griz.

The big bear had spent several hours over those night shifts with me, helping clean out the carburetors and replace all of the old gas lines, mount some fresh tires, and install some modern upgrades like electric start and a more comfy saddle...I think working on the bike made him feel a little closer to a lost brother. I have to admit, I felt a decent amount of bonding between him and I over the blood and sweat that was being poured into that bike. No tears though; real men don't cry. It was nice to see the big guy soften up a little. He also shared stories of my old man that I'd never heard before; like how one night when they were leaving the bar, they pulled out of the parking lot and drove up to a red light.

"Apparently, we had a little more to drink that night than I realized because when we came to a stop, you could tell that your dad never even considered the idea of putting his feet down and his bike tipped over with him on board!" Griz exclaimed before breaking into a fit of laughter. "His ankle got pinned underneath the bike making him unable to get out from underneath it, and I was too busy laughing my ass off to offer much help, so he just had to lie on the ground until I could regain enough of my wits to lift the 800 pound monster off of him."

I couldn't help but chuckle a little bit from the mental image of somebody pulling up to a red light and slowly tipping over because they're too sloshed to put their feet down.

"Another time, Lee was messing with Riot when Riot was just a prospect – making him stand perfectly still while your dad shot the ground in front of Riot's feet just to see how close he could get without Riot flinching."

Guns, drugs, and alcohol don't go together, folks.

"Evidently, your old man got a little too close with his last shot and blew a hole in the tip of Riot's leather boot. Luckily, the boot was a little big and had just enough space that the bullet went completely through without hitting any flesh."

That might explain why Riot hasn't shown any interest in chatting with me much.

"Riot keeps those beat up old shoes on a shelf behind his chair in the meeting room at the clubhouse. I think he uses them to serve as a reminder of his unflinching dedication to the club and his position."

It was about that time that Griz and I heard the tell-tale sound of chain-link fence rattling. Griz gave me a quizzical glance, and without even thinking my instincts and training kicked in. I took off around the corner of the garage in a dead sprint and locked my gaze onto the back of an average built male. It only took a couple seconds and a matter of fifty feet for me to catch up and tackle the intruder. As I got within a few feet of him, I lowered my shoulder and lunged for his lower back, sending him face first into the far corner of the building. He bounced off of the concrete structure like a rag doll, hitting the ground with a moan, his face gushing blood from a shattered nose.

Once I had him on the ground, I flipped him over onto his back so I could see who I was dealing with. After being gone for six years, I probably wouldn't have recognized very many people in the first place, but since this dude appeared to be all of 18 years old, you can bet there was no way I had a clue who he was.

On the other hand, when Griz finally caught up to all the action, there was no hesitation identifying the young intruder. He reached down with his huge, bear-like paws and snatched the kid up by his shirt collar. "I'm pretty sure I've given you clear instructions to stay off my property. What wasn't clear when I said, 'Stay off my property' the last time I caught your ass?" The grizzled biker reached into the kid's front pocket and pulled out a bag of white powder. He opened the bag and dumped the contents onto the ground.

"Hey man! That's mine!" was the only contribution the guy made to the conversation. Before he could get much further, Griz ripped into him once more.

"I told you once I better not catch you around here with this shit anymore, didn't I?" Griz didn't wait for a response. "This is strike 2. If I EVER see you around my place again, you'll leave in an ambulance." Faster than my brain could register, Griz threw a tremendous right hook to the left side of the kid's face. I swear I could hear his cheek bone crumble. I'm no doctor, but I've been in enough fist fights to know the sound of bone fracturing. The young punk crumpled to the ground like a sack of potatoes with a moan that was barely audible.

"Will, help me get this piece of trash off my property," was the last thing Griz said about this little encounter. He grabbed the kid under his arms, I picked up his feet and we heaved the poor bastard back across the metal mesh that he had just climbed over a couple moments ago. That's when we walked back to the garage and left the dude there, lying on the ground in a heap.

I knew going in that I would have to turn my morals way down, it's not like I was going to be selling Girl Scout cookies, but I was not prepared to witness a kid's face getting caved in and being left to take care of himself. I knew this club was a cancer to this town, but seeing the effect first-hand was jarring. Possibly the most surprising thing to me was how little I felt about what had just happened. Maybe the club was already affecting me, or maybe it had something to do with the kid being a druggy, but normally I would at least make sure he wasn't choking to death on his own blood.

Chapter 6

Time to make my first drop. This wasn't nerve-wracking at all. I'm just kidding; it couldn't have been any more stressful. I really didn't expect the Kings to have any suspicions since I'd only been in town for little more than a week, but all it takes is somebody seeing you leaving a wrapped package in a trash can for them to get a little curious.

I chose to do my business in the early morning. I figured most people would still be in bed, but there would be enough movement with early risers going to work that I wouldn't stand out too much and draw unwanted attention. Also, the vast majority of the club would still be sleeping off their hangovers.

I decided to take my truck since it is infinitely quieter than the rumbling exhaust of a motorcycle, and the last thing I want to do is raise suspicion of any of my activities. Plus, it's not nearly as recognizable in case somebody familiar would happen to spot me out and about at 5:00 in the morning.

I pulled out of my apartment complex, and headed for the tiny "downtown" area of Rough River Falls. I passed the dead end that the MC resided on, affectionately known around town as Clubhouse Road. As I expected, it looked completely deserted. A few blocks later I passed Griz's Garage before finally reaching Main Street. I hung a left and parked on the far side of the Gas N' Go. The restrooms were on the outside of the building, and there was a trash can that was obscured from view that nobody paid any attention to. You might think making a drop at the only gas station in town might be a little "high profile" for someone not wanting to raise suspicions. But to the contrary; by stopping at the only business in town that's open that early in the morning, throwing away a plastic bag full of "trash" then wandering inside to get a donut, I blended in perfectly. Yeah yeah, I'm a cop getting a donut. Call it cliché if you must, I don't care. Donuts are delicious whether you're a cop or not.

Surprisingly, I had already gathered quite a bit of useful information. I imagine a lot of my intel wasn't anything new – the DEA already had to know quite a bit of the club's structure, I was just confirming it. It's not like they hadn't already done some preliminary recon from afar. They had to get this case organized and on track while they were waiting on my recruitment. However, having a better idea of the size of the club is definitely not something they could have known.

One thing they probably didn't expect though, was the admission of my first offense. They're smart enough to know that I would have to participate in some criminal activity to really sell my cover and show the Kings how sincere I was about joining the MC. I had to be careful, because it's not like I was given a free pass to break any and every law I wanted, but if I had to snort a line of cocaine to prove my allegiance or test the product, then they knew to look the other way. If I was in a situation where I had to kick a little ass, then it's not like I had to sweat about catching a battery charge. However, I don't think the Agency was expecting me to get so involved so quickly. That's they're fault; we're talking about outlaw bikers here. The thing I was most worried about was losing myself in the club. I couldn't allow the Kings to break my morals, even if I already knew I would have to bend them throughout this investigation.

I'm not sure about the Agency's expectations regarding my connections though. In some aspects, I felt that my investigation was developing pretty quickly with how easy it was to rekindle some old relationships inside the Kings. On the other hand, the cold shoulder I was getting from Riot, and subsequently Mack, was delaying my homecoming more than I had hoped, which was frustrating. Riot's newer minions also took his lead and were hesitant to warm up to me. The older guys who were more established in the club felt freer to welcome me back without the Prez's official approval though.

For being my first drop, I think things went smoothly. I did my best to plan accordingly and picked an inconspicuous place at a favorable time of day. What I didn't plan on was Mack being an early bird. I stepped out the front door of the convenience store and bumped right into the Kings enforcer. Because I hadn't been paying attention, seeing the club's colors right in front of my face made my heart skip a beat. I looked Mack in the eye, trying to hide the panicked frenzy in my own eyes. "Hey Mack, sorry about that. You're up awfully early today, huh?" Nervously, I found myself fidgeting with my hands, naturally popping my knuckles to try to look as collected as possible.

"Yeah, couldn't sleep last night so I figured I might as well go for a ride and see if that might help clear my mind a little bit. Got a lot going on, you know?" He was uncharacteristically friendly this morning. "What are you doing out and about at this time of morning?" he asked, slightly squinting his eyes out of suspicion.

I had to think quickly. Luckily, I had the perfect excuse ingrained in my DNA from the past six years. "Up at 0500 every day. That's what the military'll do to you. Is your stuff anything I can help with?" I figured I might as well offer and see if he might open up a little bit. Never hurts to try, especially when you're trying to make connections.

"Not really man. Club stuff. Nothing that needs to be discussed with outsiders," was his curt response. And just like that, any glimmer of hope I had of trying to break the ice with him was gone. I guess on the bright side, his cold shoulder kept him from asking any questions about me and what I was up to.

"Fair enough, I can understand that. I'll see you around then." I left it at that. I didn't want to pry and get caught fishing for too much information, so I tried my best to play it cool. At this point I had no affiliation with the Kings what-so-ever, so I honestly had no business knowing anything about the club at all.

Chapter 7

The next few weeks were a little frustrating. With the work on dad's bike being done, I really didn't have an excuse to hang around the garage anymore, so I had to come up with another tactic to be around the club. It's not like I could just show up to the clubhouse and expect to hang out, so I tried the next best thing. The clubhouse was always fully stocked with alcohol, but bikers aren't typically known for the culinary skills. Therefore, luckily for me, several of them spent a lot of time at Rusty's Tavern about a block down from the Gas N' Go. Technically, the name of the Tavern was currently Breakers Bar and Grill, but there had been so many different owners and name changes over the years that the locals got tired of trying to remember which incarnation was up and running, so they reverted to the original name and stuck with it. Useless trivia aside, the menu was quite impressive and you couldn't make a bad choice.

Being a bachelor, it didn't seem unusual that I ate so many meals at the tavern, which worked out well because I could catch RJ for lunch, Griz for dinner, and whoever else that might be with them. I got to know El C a little more, and it became clear that he was the most responsible member of the Kings and being the road captain was an obvious role for him. He was actually a banker by day and led a pretty normal lifestyle. His old lady was the only librarian on staff at the town's library. That might explain the club's willingness to volunteer there so much.

Before long, I needed to develop my cover a little more. I had been in town for a couple of weeks and needed a job to give the appearance that I was trying to make a living. After so long without work, people start wondering where your income comes from, and the last thing I need is somebody looking into me too closely. Luckily, with all of the time I was spending at the tavern, I was able to secure a part-time bartending gig.

Also around that time, I started noticing Kayla. I had gone to school with her when we were younger, but evidently she waited for me to leave for the Air Force before she fully blossomed (if you catch my drift). She worked as a waitress at the tavern, so I had plenty opportunity to make a new impression. She seemed friendly enough, but I couldn't get a clear reading as to whether she was interested in me or not. I noticed little things; like how she'd put her hand on my shoulder when she'd come to the table to get my order, or hold my eye contact and smile just a second longer than somebody normally would otherwise. Seems pretty clear, right? But other times, I would reciprocate the flirting and get shot down in flames – hard.

After several trips to the tavern and working some shifts behind the bar, getting mixed signals from Kayla basically helped me decide that I was tired of the mind games. I wasn't gonna let some girl that I barely remembered from high school drive me insane. That's when she sauntered over to my booth. I was sitting on the edge, next to the aisle when she walked up and stopped next to me. She rested her hip against my shoulder and asked what I wanted. Since I had already made up my mind that I wasn't going to entertain her anymore, I restrained from making eye contact. That hardly means that I could resist sneaking a peak at her from the corner of my eye. She was standing right next to me – *leaning* on me for crying out loud. As nonchalantly as possible, I let my eyes wander to the limits of their sockets. I was still doing my best to restrain myself, so I was trying to take everything in through my periphery. Her presence was hard to ignore.

Temptation finally got the best of me. I couldn't hold out any longer and caved in. I turned my head in her direction, first noticing the way her hair fell down onto her shoulders before my eyes snapped up to meet hers. Totally busted.

She flashed a coy little grin, then asked again, "What can I do for you tonight, hun?"

She had no idea what kind of filthy things flowed through my head. "Just let me get a hot ham and cheese sandwich with a glass of sweet tea. No lemon," was my business-like response.

After several minutes, Kayla strutted back in my direction with a cup of tea and my order in her hands. She sat the cup and plate on the table, then sat down directly across from me. After I started eating she asked if everything tasted okay and leaned onto the table. I decided there had been enough cat and mouse. It was time to lay it on the table. "Kayla, when are you gonna let me take you out?" I asked.

"All you had to do was ask."

Her response almost made my head explode. I was exasperated. "Then why have you been so hot and cold with me?!" I blurted out. "Every time I think I get you, that's when you give me the cold shoulder!"

"What can I say? A girl can get a little frustrated after all that flirting and you not taking the hint." She left her explanation at that.

My mouth had dried out a little, so I took a deep swig from the glass of sweet tea sitting in front of me. "So what time do you get off work?"

She squinted her eyes at me, playing coy, as she stood up from the booth. "Pick me up here at 8:30." And with that, she walked off.

Chapter 8

I rumbled up to the front of the tavern on my bike a few minutes before 8:30. You couldn't have missed her standing at the corner of the building from across town.

Kayla stood straight with her weight on her left leg, her right leg slightly bent. She must have brought her intuition expecting to ride on my bike because she chose to wear knee high leather boots as opposed to sandals or heels. Her left hand was resting on her hip and her right arm dangled loosely. Her dark brown, wavy hair cascaded down to the middle of her back. It's hard to imagine a woman that looks like that living in anonymity in the middle of nowhere.

After my bike came to a stop, she strutted over, kicked her right leg over the seat and straddled the rear fender, leaning back against the high-rise sissy bar. I offered a spare helmet that I had brought with me, but women like Kayla aren't usually interested in helmet hair…especially not when it could just as easily be flowing in the wind. I walked the bike back away from the curb, pointed it toward the street, eased out on the clutch, and rolled on the throttle. Kayla leaned forward, resting on my back, choosing to use me for balance instead of the sissy bar. I didn't mind.

We roared down Main Street past the Gas N' Go on our way out of town. It took less than a minute before we reached the edge of town and Main Street turned into Highway 54. I don't normally have passengers when I ride, but having Kayla draped across my back felt right. After a few miles, I leaned to my right and rolled the bike through the Highway 54 - 110 split. Once the bike returned upright after coming through the curve, I felt Kayla lean back away from me. I turned my head to see her tilt her chin up, close her eyes, and raise her arms straight out to her sides to soak up the freedom. Nothing compares to being on a bike.

It wasn't long before we came to Rough River Falls State Park. I slowed our momentum to make the turn into the entrance and kept it in low gear to make the climb up the very steep hill leading to the landing area at the top. I found a good parking spot and dropped the kickstand before leading Kayla toward the deserted picnic area. I grabbed hold of one of the picnic tables and drug it next to the railing of the overlook area. I swept all of the crumbs and dirt off the top of the table with my hand, then took a seat and invited Kayla to join me.

"I don't know why nobody ever comes up here," I pondered out loud. I never gave it much thought, but now that I was there I realized how true that was. Even before I picked Kayla up, I fully expected to have the place all to ourselves. I looked out from the overlook and took in the sun setting over the falls of the Rough River. Beyond the northern banks was green Kentucky farmland as far as you could see, with some rolling hills on the horizon. The waning sun plastered the sky from yellow to orange to blue, then purple. There was a light breeze that made the trees dance around us. It was perfect.

"People are too busy and self-absorbed to realize the beauty this place has to offer I think," came Kayla's response. "Also, I still think there's a stigma this place has."

"Stigma?"

"Yeah. A sign of disgrace or infamy."

What a smartass. "Oh, right...*that* stigma," I sarcastically replied. "Why does this place have a stigma?"

"I keep forgetting you haven't been around here for awhile. This is where that Olsen boy OD'd a few months ago," she explained.

Of course I was aware of that, but playing dumb about that situation served me a lot better at this point.

"That was really big news around here for quite awhile. Any unnatural death around here is big news, but especially with it being a State Representative's kid. It must've given people the impression that this park is where druggies go to get high."

I just sat quietly, listening intently.

"Stellar date conversation, huh?" she quipped.

As twilight progressed we stayed on the picnic table, shifting every once in awhile to find a more comfortable position on the hard surface. Kayla carried most of the conversation, filling me in on what's been going on in the years I've been M.I.A. "The drug scene here has gotten pretty bad. The MC is to blame for almost all of it. It didn't surprise many people when somebody turned up dead, they were only surprised about who it was. I think most people realized it was only a matter of time. I'm just glad it wasn't my brother..." She trailed off at the end.

"You have a brother?" I asked.

"Oh come on," she answered. "He was only a couple years younger than us in school. He's prospecting with the Kings now."

All of a sudden, the realization slapped me across the face. Kayla's brother is the prospect that unloaded my dad's, err – my bike from the trailer when I first pulled into Griz's Garage.

"He's been prospecting with them for about two years. I think they enjoy keeping him around just so they have somebody they can treat like garbage; otherwise wouldn't they have already patched him in by now?"

Two years is a long time to prospect – typically a club knows by then whether a prospect can cut it or not, and if not then they turn him loose.

"What you said earlier," I interrupted, redirecting the conversation to something a little more useful, "about being glad it wasn't your brother that OD'd. What's his story?" I asked out of genuine curiosity, but also because I'm sure having a little back-story could serve me well down the line.

"Our mom and dad were killed in a car accident when he was a senior," she began. "I had been out of school for a couple years and already had my own place and a job, so naturally he moved in with me. I guess in my head, I had the thought that I would take care of him until he graduated and found his own job, but he coped a little differently than I did. I leaned on responsibility to help keep my head on straight, but he totally fell apart. He skipped school more than he went until he finally dropped out altogether, and he started using whatever drugs and alcohol he could get his hands on. That's where his interaction with the Kings began. He hung around outside the tavern waiting for anybody from the club to stop in, and when they did he bought out whatever they had on them. His habit eventually led to cocaine. I tried to intervene, but he was beyond my help – I figured it was only a matter of time until he joined mom and dad, and I think that's what he was going for."

"So what happened?"

"I don't know. One night I came home from work and he was sitting on my couch. His eyes were red, puffy, and bloodshot, but not like he was high. I was kind of confused, and I just stood in the doorway and kind of stared at him for a few minutes. He tried to look at me, but when we made eye contact he started crying. We talked that whole night about everything. He said he didn't know what he was supposed to do with himself when mom and dad died. He just wanted to forget everything and feel happy, you know? He decided that night to clean himself up and he hasn't touched drugs since. I think the Kings noticed a dip in sales because it wasn't long before they asked him to prospect. I don't think they liked the idea of losing one of their best customers, so they figured they'd reel him back in. After being a hang-around for so long, he jumped at the chance to be a real part of the club. He was excited to get that black and blue patch on his back someday, but all they've done is treat him like dirt. They call him 'Junky' for Christ's sake. Some friends, huh?"

"So why does he stick around then?" I asked. "If they treat him so bad, why does he keep tolerating it?"

"Because he doesn't have anything. I tried my best to take care of him, but my salary from the tavern isn't enough to support two people…it's barely enough to support me, and if it wasn't for the apartment above the tavern, it probably *wouldn't* support me. Plus, nobody wants to hire somebody with track marks up and down their arms, either. The club gives him a small room in the back of the clubhouse with a cot, and a little money to fill his stomach. In exchange, all he has to do is take all their shit and keep the clubhouse relatively clean."

I couldn't resist the feeling of pity that was creeping in for her brother. We sat in the park and talked for hours. When we started to run out of things to talk about, I looked out and saw the earliest light of dawn creeping up the horizon. I stood up to stretch my legs and held out my hand. Kayla looked at me for a second – I could see in her eyes that she was wondering what I was up to. Eventually, she surrendered and put her hand in mine. Without a word, I led her back to my bike. We rode out of the park and spent the sunrise in the wind. I dropped her back off in front of the tavern right at 8:30 in the morning. And *that* my friends, is a date!

Chapter 9

I drug myself into the tavern that night for my shift, feeling exhausted after a nap that morning and afternoon. Okay, fine, I guess *technically* it was a full night's worth of sleep, but my schedule was still flipped upside-down so my body was rebelling against me a little bit. "You look like hell," one of the other bartenders confirmed. Kayla was lucky enough to have the day off. Too bad, because I wouldn't mind watching her strut around all night.

My shift crawled by, my fatigue making it feel even slower than normal, until a couple of the Kings came in. It was close to midnight when Riot and Mack strolled in. They walked over to me and grabbed a stool at the bar.

"What's going on guys?" A good bartender has to be skilled at small talk. "Anything good?"

"Depends, I guess," was Riot's reply. "Some of the guys have been talking around the clubhouse, talking about me maybe coming down here and talking to you."

"Oh yeah?" I was honestly surprised.

"The discussion has come up more than once that some of the old-timers like your company and think you'd fit in with us a little bit. I'm not so sure, but we'll see if that changes."

"Here," Mack said simply, and tossed a leather vest *at* me – not *to* me. "Put that on. See how it feels."

I couldn't hide the grin from forming at the corners of my mouth. I held up the back of the vest to reveal the lone rocker patch at the top. The arched black and blue patch read Kings of Chaos. The plain vest signified a great deal – I was now prospecting for the club and was at their mercy 24/7. I swung it around my back and slid my arms through the openings, choosing to leave the front unbuttoned since I wasn't currently on the move. "Feels good!"

Riot looked me in the eye and left our conversation with two simple sentences: "You're official now. Anything, anywhere, anytime."

And with that he and Mack turned to leave the bar. Before they got to the door though, Mack bumped into a patron who had wobbled into his path. Mack grabbed the guys' shirt collar and gave him a firm shove out of the way. When the guy took exception to the rough treatment Mack ended the confrontation before it could start, snapping his left hand squarely into the drunk's mouth without even breaking stride for the exit. The guy dropped to the floor in a puddle of spilled beer…at least I hope for his sake it was beer!

Once the guy regained some of his wits, he made a bee-line straight for the bar with his eyes locked on me. "What are you gonna do about this??" Blood leaked from a gash in his top lip. He spit a pool of blood onto the bar along with a small chunk of his tongue, apparently bitten off when he was punched.

"I'm gonna have you get the hell outta my bar, is what I'm gonna do, before you bleed all over it!"

"You're not gonna call the cops?" he asked, incredulously.

"Sure, what do you want me to tell them? That you're too drunk to stay out of people's way? They were just walking out when you invaded their space – that's how I saw it. Now how 'bout this; you go ahead and get outta here before I decide to reenact the scene?" I was given the vest, now it was time to play the part. Afraid of a second altercation, the guy scuttled out of the bar with his tail tucked between his legs. It was slightly scary how quickly my personality picked up tendencies from the club.

46

Chapter 10

The end of my shift flew by. Whether it was the high from getting my official invite from the Kings or the adrenaline remaining from Mack's dust-up with the drunkard, I was floating on cloud nine. As soon as I could usher out the last few customers after last call and lock the door behind them, I hopped on my bike and drove straight to the clubhouse.

Griz and RJ were standing outside when I rolled up and they greeted me with big smiles and warm hugs. "Hey brother!" RJ welcomed me. "Wanna grab me a beer?" He patted me on the back and ushered me toward the front door of the clubhouse.

"Hey, get one for me too, prospect!" Griz ordered playfully.

Once I stepped foot in the clubhouse for the first time, my head almost started spinning. I had already gained the trust of this very motley crew and been welcomed into their world. Also, I was one step closer to fulfilling my mission with the DEA. The walls were plastered with picture frames displaying photos featuring original members, current members, and members who had passed, as well as mugshots and group shots from organized rides. In the back corner was a card table where a heated game of poker was being played. Along the far wall were the double doors, adorned with the skull and V-Twin crown logo that presumably led to the official meeting room. I hesitantly wandered behind the bar, making sure I didn't piss anyone off for being somewhere I wasn't supposed to be. Wouldn't you know it, before I could get back to RJ and Griz, every member was lined up by the bar waiting to be served; I ended one shift at a bar just to start another one…fabulous.

It wasn't long after when Kayla's brother strolled over to me. "Did ya forget about Griz and RJ standing out there? They said they've been waiting on you for their drinks. Probably not a good idea to piss off patch members already," he said rather snarky. I guess even tenured prospects get to pull rank on me. Sensing that he was going to get the night off since I was the new guy, he snatched a bottle from the fridge and wandered down the back hallway where, I assume, his room was located.

By the time the night wound down and I had the bar in order, I started to make my way outside toward my bike. The sun was already starting to come up – I guess this is my schedule now. If I was quick, I could get back to my apartment, update my status, and make my next drop before it got much later. However, when I rolled into the parking lot of my apartment complex I knew it wouldn't be that easy. I had come to know my loser neighbor from living next door and being around the club. The guys called him "Stitch" due to his skin being so mangled and scarred from numerous bike wrecks resulting in broken bones and surgery. He was laying on the concrete walkway, his head and shoulders propped against the front door of his apartment.

"Hey Stitch, long night?" I asked.

"Shut it, smartass. The old lady's bent outta shape and won't let me in."

"Come on man, you can crash on my couch." I stuck out my hand, offering to help him up off of the ground. I hated the thought, but as a brand new prospect, I had a duty to fulfill. I opened my front door and Stitch headed straight for the couch. "The bathroom's down the hall on the right."

"I know where the bathroom is. I live right next door – my apartment looks just like yours."

"I highly doubt that," I mumbled to myself. I walked into my bedroom and pushed the door closed but didn't latch it so I could listen to his movement. I opened my laptop and prepared the files needed to make my drop. I feverishly typed the updates and new happenings so I could be done with it. By the time I had finished, Stitch was out cold in my living room, sawing logs like nobody's business.

I carefully and quietly tiptoed out of my apartment, trying not to wake him. I stepped out through the storm door when I turned around to pull the front door closed. I didn't hear Stitch get up, but when I turned he was standing right in front of me.

"Where are you sneaking off to?" he demanded.

I could feel my heart jump into my throat. My palms felt clammy, filled with nervous sweat. Like second nature, I reached for my knuckles to start popping them, but my hands were too slippery from all the moisture. I tried to calm myself the best I could before I answered, luckily he couldn't see my veins pounding out my pulse. "I'm not sneaking anywhere, man. I have some errands to run and was trying not to wake you up." I had taped the flash drive containing my information to the inside of a styrofoam cup so it looked like I was just carrying around a fountain pop. Luckily the disguise was adequate and Stitch didn't think twice about my beverage. "If you don't mind, I have shit to do. Make yourself comfy and sleep as long as you need." With that I spun away from him and marched straight for my pickup. When I backed out of the parking spot and directed the truck toward the road, I couldn't help but notice Stitch still standing in my doorway watching me as I left. "What a creep," I said to myself as I pulled out of the parking lot and into the street.

This time, due to the time being a little later than I had hoped for and more people being out and about, I had to use the secondary location that had been designated as a drop-off zone. I came to a stop in the parking lot facing the town's tiny park. The park was about the size of a block, and had a baseball field to my right occupying roughly half the area. The other half had a less-than-regulation size basketball court, jungle gym, slide, and rusted out swing set. To my immediate left was a small concession stand that hadn't been open in my lifetime and to the far side of that was a bench that faced into the park.

I strolled over to the bench and had a seat, casually looking around to see if

I had any admirers. The park was abandoned and it was apparently still too early for the residents of the trailer park across the street to be out and about. Once my butt occupied the bench, I nonchalantly leaned forward, resting my elbows on my knees. I discreetly popped the lid off the Styrofoam cup and pulled the flash drive out. I tore a fresh piece of tape from a small roll in my vest pocket, then secured the device to the bottom of the bench. I sat there for several minutes to give the impression that I was just out for some fresh air just in case anybody happened to be watching. In the distance I heard the roar of a V-twin. Son of a – where do these guys keep coming from?! I guess I shouldn't be too surprised though, in a town this small you're bound to run into people frequently. Seconds later, RJ pulled into the parking lot next to my truck and dropped his kickstand. He walked in my direction, so I stood to greet him.

"Hey prospect, what are you doing out here?"

"Really, RJ? You gotta start in with this prospect stuff too?"

"That's your title, isn't it?" he asked seriously.

Nevermind the history we have with each other, I guess. I reluctantly nodded my head in response. "Just thought I'd get out and enjoy a little quiet time. Stitch is currently laid out on my couch and he's making it sound like there's a helicopter circling my apartment."

"Stitch," RJ scoffed. "One of the Kings' finest," he said, accompanied with an eye roll. "That's one of Riot's boys right there. None of us can figure out Riot's game plan – why he brings in guys like that. The only thing I can guess is Riot is scared of people who can think for themselves. That's why he surrounds himself with 'yes men' like Stitch and Mack…what those guys lack in brains, they make up for in loyalty."

"RJ, let me ask you something," I butted in. "Speaking of Mack, what is his and Riot's deal with me?"

"I think Riot is threatened by you to be perfectly honest with you, and Mack will go along with whatever Riot says or does. Since Riot took over the club he makes sure nothing happens without his knowledge or involvement. When you showed up, a lot of the old-timers wanted to welcome you in right away and I don't think Riot really cared for the sentiment because it wasn't his idea. He *says* his reluctance is because he's a little worried about your background, but I think that's just a smokescreen to hide his real concern which is with the way the old members naturally respond to you."

Uh-oh. Even if it is a smokescreen, any mention of my background with the Air Force makes me a little uneasy. "I'd think there are enough guys that know me and can vouch for me that would ease Riot's tension," I offered, trying to gloss over the situation.

"Need a refill?" RJ glanced down to my empty cup. His eyes lingered on it for a second until I realized the lid was still unsealed and just resting loosely on top of the cup. I tried to tilt the cup so he couldn't see the small piece of tape still dangling inside the container.

"Nah, after last night what I need to do is quit it with the caffeine and hit the sack. I'll catch up with you and the guys later, RJ." With that, I stood and started walking toward my truck. I pushed the lid down on the cup and tossed it in a trash can that was sitting close to my pickup, hoping that RJ wouldn't think anything of it. As I drove away I tried to keep an eye on my mirrors to see if RJ made any move; he didn't. I don't know how many more drops I can make before I go into full-blown cardiac arrest…this shit is stressful!

Wouldn't you know it, when I approached my apartment complex I could clearly see my front door standing wide open. This day was never going to end. I swung my truck into the parking spot and jammed on the brakes. I hopped out of the cab and swiftly walked across the lawn before stopping right outside of my door. I cocked my head and just listened for several seconds. When I didn't hear anything, I decided to check things out. Quietly, I stepped through the threshold and glanced into the kitchen area behind me before focusing on the living room directly in front of me. I didn't see or hear anybody, but I did notice a couple glaring differences from when I left. First, Stitch was gone. Second, there was white powder all over my coffee table and I highly doubt he was eating powdered donuts before he left. Lastly, I noticed that my fairly extensive movie collection had been raided and close to half of them were gone. A quick survey of the rest of the apartment assured me that nothing else was out of order, so I decided to have a little chat with my neighbor.

I marched over to Stitch's apartment and pounded on his front door. His old lady answered the door and she brought her attitude with her. "What do you want, pounding on the door like you're the po-lice?"

"Let me talk to Stitch," I answered impatiently. I still had to be somewhat respectful due to my lowly stature with the club, but it's just his old lady – not like I'm talking to a patch member or anything.

"What do you want, prospect?" came a yell from the living room.

I looked past the haggard mess standing in front of me and spotted Stitch kicked back on their couch. "I noticed my apartment was a little different than it was before I left. Wanted to see if you knew anything about it."

"Depends on what you're talking about."

My patience was running thin. "I'm talking about the coke on my coffee table and all the missing movies from my shelf."

"Oh, that? I just borrowed a couple movies man, no big deal," he casually replied.

"And the coke??" I snapped at him.

"You said to make yourself comfortable, remember?"

"Either clean up your mess when you're done or leave enough for me.

Come on, man." I tried to mellow out and let him know that I had no problem being around the powder and tried to imply that I wanted to be around more of it.

He raised an eyebrow in interest, but didn't say anything. He nodded his head a few times as he turned his attention back to the TV. Finally…contact. His old lady closed the door in front of me, but not before I saw the small boy streak through the living room in nothing but a diaper. I could've sworn he had a pair of scissors. I was starting to feel desperate for this kid. There's no way he stood a chance.

Chapter 11

I slept the day away, trying to recover from the past couple of nights. I got to the tavern for my shift, unsure of whether Kayla would be working or not to keep me distracted. Luckily, when I walked through the door I immediately spotted the brunette beauty. There she stood in all her glory. Suddenly, walking across the room became a lot trickier, if you catch my drift. Wink, wink, nudge, nudge. When the bell attached to the door rang, she turned her head from the table of patrons she was waiting on to see who was coming in. When she saw it was me I noticed a small smile cross her lips. Just as quickly, I noticed that smile disappear just before she turned away.

Once I got settled in behind the bar, I turned my focus to grabbing Kayla's attention. I'm not sure why, but it really seemed like she was going out of her way to avoid me. For as difficult as it was just to ask her out, I don't know why I thought it would be less complicated now that we'd actually gone out. Sooner than later somebody needed a drink so she was forced to talk to me. My attempt at idle chit chat went unreturned as she grabbed the glass from the bar and walked away. Eventually, I caught her at the end of the bar while she was taking a break.

"Hey, got a minute?" I gingerly asked. She glanced up at me, frost in her glare. "Why the cold shoulder treatment tonight?" I followed up. "I thought the other night went well and we both had a good time?"

"It has nothing to do with the other night," she corrected me. "It has everything to do with what you're wearing."

I could only assume she was referring to the vest. "Listen, Kayla," I started. "Me wearing this vest doesn't change anything between you and me. It doesn't change who I am or anything else."

"Maybe not yet...." She murmured.

I reached out and placed my hand on top of hers. She looked up and met my gaze. "Don't worry," I assured her. "I can handle this." She gave me a weak smile before standing up and returning to work.

*****

Once last call came and went, I got the bar cleaned up and locked down. Kayla's attitude toward me had thawed a little throughout the night, but she still hadn't warmed up to me like I wanted. After I wiped all of the spilt beer off of the bar, I noticed Kayla starting up the stairs in the back of the kitchen that led to her apartment. "Hey!" I quickly yelled at her. "Come here." When she got a little closer, I started walking toward the front door. "Let's go for a ride."

We mounted the old Harley and I started heading out of town on Highway 54. Just like last time, I leaned the bike to the right to make the gradual curve onto Highway 110 at the 54-110 split. Again, I started to brake before the entrance to Rough River Falls State Park, only this time I turned left across traffic. Slowly, I crept along the gravel road that led down to the bank of the Rough River. Riding on gravel is never fun, so I was really focusing on keeping the bike steady…especially since I had Kayla sitting behind me, her arms wrapped around my waist to try to absorb a little body heat and block some of the wind. Temperatures coming off the water can get a little brisk at 5:00 a.m. The gravel road opened up into a grassy clearing about three-quarters of a mile off the highway. Once I parked the bike and Kayla hopped off, I took the blanket that I keep strapped to the front of my handlebars to use as a bedroll, and unraveled it on the grass so we'd have some place to sit and get comfortable.

We sat in silence for a couple minutes. She was unsure of why I brought her here and I was unsure of how to start. I started to open my mouth a couple different times, but didn't know what to say until I finally looked Kayla in the eye. "Don't let this vest fool you. This doesn't make me any different from two days ago. I'm not wearing it for the same reasons as the other guys."

"Then why *are* you wearing it?" she probed.

"It's more of a tribute in a way. A way to fix the family that I never really had. By wearing this, maybe I'll feel a connection to my old man that was never there when I was little." Yeah, that sounded good.

"That's what my brother was looking for. Look how that's turned out for him," she shot back.

"I'm thinking that maybe I can make life a little easier for your brother. With my connections and history with a lot of those guys, I should be able to influence things a little bit. A major angle for me is to try to get them to back off your brother. There's nothing I can do about it tonight or tomorrow, but maybe in the not-too-distant future I'll have a little power of persuasion. If nothing else, maybe he'll catch a little break simply because he isn't the lowest man on the totem pole anymore."

I could see the skepticism all over her face which made it really hard to recognize the gratitude in her eyes. After a moment of silence, she leaned in to me and planted a kiss on my lips. She pulled back slightly and let her lips linger just out of reach of mine to see how I would react. I quickly leaned forward before she could pull back any further. Satisfied with our first and second kisses, we moved on to round three which turned out even better. We gradually laid back onto the blanket, acting like we were a couple of high schoolers. After our blood returned to other areas of our bodies, we laid on the blanket and gazed up at the sky before eventually deciding to head back to town.

When we coasted into the parking lot of the tavern Kayla loosened her grip around my waist. The cool night air made her cling to me for warmth and I didn't mind the least bit. After she dismounted from the bike, I grabbed her hand and pulled her in for another kiss before she started to walk away. Once she was a few steps away, she turned back and gave me a playful look. "You coming?" That's all I needed to hear before killing the engine and following her inside.

Chapter 12

I awoke late that morning to voices coming from the other room. Kayla was clearly one of them, but I wasn't sure whose male voice I was hearing. Was she really so bold to have another guy in her apartment while I slept in her bed? I grabbed my jeans from beside the bed and slid them on, not wasting time with the zipper or button, then threw on my t-shirt and grabbed my vest before cautiously padding closer to the bedroom door. Wouldn't you know it, about two-thirds of the way to the door the floor creaked under my shifting weight. Some undercover agent I am! I decided there was no reason to try to be stealthy anymore, so I stepped into the door frame to get a good look at my competition. One thing I had going for me was intimidation; I'm sure whoever was here saw my bike sitting out front and I wasn't trying to hide my vest, holding it to my side, making sure it was visible to Kayla's company. Unfortunately, the guy I was staring at couldn't care less about me being a biker since he was wearing an identical vest. Her brother glared at me like I had just dishonored his family. I guess in a way, he was kind of right.

"Where's your phone?" he demanded. "The guys have been trying to call you for the last couple hours. They got tired of waiting and sent me out to hunt you down. Get to the clubhouse, now."

I checked my cell phone that had been in my front jeans pocket – 6 missed calls. "Oh shit," was all I could get out before my stomach dropped and a nervous feeling crashed into me like a tidal wave. I rushed out the door and down the front steps leading to a door just to the side of the tavern where my bike had been parked. I managed to say a quick goodbye to Kayla on my way out and assured her that I would catch up to her later, once I took care of whatever business needed to be taken care of.

All the way to the clubhouse, I felt like I was walking into a trap that I was wildly unprepared for. My unsnapped vest was open and flapping in the breeze, my boots were untied and I still hadn't even fastened my pants before firing up my bike and booking it to the dead-end on Clubhouse Road. I pulled up to the domicile and parked among the multitude of bikes sitting out front. On my way through the front door, I buttoned my jeans and buckled my belt. Mack was standing front and center once I stepped in and gained my bearings…great.

"Meeting room," was all he said. His tone let me know my presence today was all business.

All I could keep thinking about was how in the hell did they find out who I was? How was I going to get out of this? My pulse was racing as fast as my mind. I stepped through the double doors adorned with the Skull King logo. I swear it was taunting me. Mack followed me in and sealed the room. A quick scan with a wand assured him that I wasn't wearing a wire. Riot was sitting at the head of the table. Mack took a seat immediately to his right, literally making him Riot's right hand man. At the other end of the table sat Stitch, with RJ sitting about halfway down the table, directly across from the double doors.

This did not look good at all. "What's going on?" I asked, trying to steel the nerves in my voice. Somehow, Stitch must've figured out what I was up to yesterday when I left him in my apartment and RJ must've confirmed it by inspecting my discarded cup at the park. Did he find the flash drive too? Now I had to answer to Riot and Mack.

"Have a seat," Riot instructed. "Stitch mentioned that you two had an interesting conversation yesterday. Have anything to add?"

"Well, I'm not sure what he told you but I really can't say anything important happened yesterday," I said, trying not to volunteer any information.

"Cut the shit, prospect," came a sneer from Stitch. "I already told them you're looking for a connection."

"Is that right?" asked Riot.

Oh right, the coke! "Yeah, I guess we had a brief discussion yesterday but it really wasn't anything. It's not like I need it. I'll quit if you're worried about it bringing attention to the club. I really didn't think it was a big deal."

"Yeah, well it *IS* kind of a big deal. In case you forgot, this town still has the Olsen shadow hanging over it," Riot admonished. "The good news is it doesn't seem like you have a big mouth and didn't try to throw Stitch under the bus when confronted. I can appreciate that. Between that and RJ pleading your case on your behalf, we decided to have a little chat today."

My pulse finally started to slow down. I looked at RJ and he looked back, nodding his head in assurance. "I'm not trying to involve myself with club business or overstep my position at all," I explained. "Stitch left behind some left-overs on my coffee table, so I just told him to leave a little more next time."

Riot looked at Mack and began slightly nodding his head. Mack stood up from his seat at Riot's side, walked over to a large metal cabinet and retrieved something but I couldn't make out what it was. When he returned to his chair he purposefully tossed a Skull King patch on the table in front of me. I was floored. Surely this wasn't their way of patching me in to the club, but it certainly seemed like it.

"That's not yours," Riot clarified. "Not yet, but it could be. We have an errand that needs taken care of. If you can complete that errand then you'll have some color added to the back of your vest. Easy enough, huh?"

I highly doubt it's gonna be that easy, but I'm in no position to squabble. "You bet," I simply responded. "Just tell me what you need and I'll make it happen."

"Pretty confident, aren't you prospect? You don't even know what we're asking yet," Riot chided.

"Irrelevant. I'll do whatever needs done. It doesn't really matter much how difficult it is." I was trying to show as much confidence and loyalty as I could muster to prove my worth to the club.

Riot looked at Mack and nodded again. This time Mack unveiled what was in his other hand. He opened his big mitt and there sat a small baggy with a white, powdery substance. "You'll do whatever needs done, huh? Prove it. Show us all how dedicated you are to this club."

By the time Riot had finished his peer pressure-filled speech, Mack had cut the coke into a couple lines. He handed me a rolled up dollar bill to use as a straw for my nose.

Just great. They had completely called my bluff, and now I was forced to show my cards and turn my bluff into a royal flush. My mind shifted into overdrive, right along with my pulse and sweat glands. I started to fidget and popped my knuckles on both hands about a dozen times each. There was no way out of this, and I couldn't afford to stall anymore. I finally steeled myself to the reality of what I was facing, and simply forced myself to act without thinking. I hunched over the table, put one end of the dollar on the table and the other end in my left nostril, used my free hand to close the empty side of my nose and sniffed. When I finished the first line, I switched the dollar to the other side and sniffed the second line. The powder coated the back of my throat and made me cough. I tried to force the coughs down so they wouldn't betray my straight-edge past. I'd never used anything harder than alcohol, and I had just snorted enough cocaine to wake up that guy from the Rolling Stones. Within minutes my senses exploded beyond comprehension.

Riot snapped his fingers in my direction to regain my attention. "You're not done. We also have a delivery that needs to be made. Sometime in the next few days you will be given some directions and a backpack. Don't get stupid when you get it. Put it on your back and take off. Keep in mind that this delivery will be time sensitive once you get it, so don't waste any. When you make the delivery you will be given another backpack. Same rules as before – don't get stupid when you get it. Put it on your back and take off. The contents of the bags are of no concern to you, so don't make it your business. If you are not given a bag in return, then do not leave the first one. After the exchange, you haul ass back here. If you screw this up, you better just keep on riding. Don't even think about coming back here – just take your headstart and pray we never catch up to you. Understood?"

I looked at Riot and nodded my head. The instructions rendered me speechless since this was the last thing I expected when I walked through the doors. Plus my thoughts were bouncing off the walls, and I couldn't corral them to offer a sensible response anyway.

"That's it," Riot finished up. "Take a good look at that patch. It's yours if you want it…all you have to do is earn it. Oh, and make sure your damn phone is on."

Once the meeting concluded, I rode back to Kayla's to try and make up for leaving her place in such haste earlier. The meeting had been all business, so it really didn't take long…all told I was only gone for maybe forty-five minutes. The ride back to her apartment was super intense. Colors were more vibrant than I had ever seen; probably because my eyes were so pegged, they were drinking in as much light as the sun had to offer. I walked in without even knocking, and was met with cold glares from Kayla and her brother. "Sorry about that," I said sheepishly to both of them.

First, I looked at Kayla to make sure she understood my delicate position with the club. Fortunately, her eyes softened a little after my apology. I think after I apologized she felt bad realizing how frantic I had been for the last hour.

"I gotta get downstairs," she said as she rounded the corner of the island separating her small dining room and kitchen. She planted a quick kiss on my lips as she passed me on her way toward the door. Once she reached for the handle she turned back and gave me a look that made me wish she had more time before her shift started at the tavern downstairs. "See you after my shift?" she asked.

"Hopefully, if some business doesn't interfere," I answered. She nodded her head back implying that she understood it was club business and was better not to ask any questions. Smart girl.

Next, I looked her brother in the eye. His gaze hadn't changed at all. I could tell he was still super-pissed that he had to track me down. Plus I just kissed his sister – that probably wasn't fun for him either. Oh well, it's his fault for still being here. Plus his sister is smoking hot.

Chapter 13

"Business, huh?" Junky asked. This was the first time he talked to me
without a shitty attitude dripping from every word. "What did they rope you into?"

"Honestly, I'm not real sure. They told me to expect some directions in the
next couple days – that's it. Until then, I'm just waiting." I wasn't too sure how
much information I should divulge. For all I knew, this could be part of the test to
see how tempted I am to run my mouth. I limited the amount of info I shared to the
bare minimum just in case, but I also wanted to get him to let down his guard a little
which is a tricky balance.

"Nice pupils," he quipped. "I recognized it the second you walked through
the door. Do they have you running a backpack?" he asked, shifting gears.

I just looked at him, unsure of how to reply.

"At least it's not me anymore," he mused. "It's kinda nice not being the
new guy any longer."

"I'll bet. How long have you been prospecting?" I asked.

"Two years, more or less. Not sure what I have left to prove at this point."

"Yeah, Kayla kinda mentioned how the club has treated you. Why do you
stick around and keep putting up with it?"

"What else am I gonna do?" came his rather blunt answer. "I doubt there
are many businesses out there looking to hire a high school dropout who fried his
brain with more chemicals than they even know exist. The Kings help me survive
even though they make my existence a living hell sometimes. I really think if I
slipped back into my old habits they'd patch me in. It's almost like they keep me
around just to tempt me. When I told them I wasn't interested in that life anymore
it's like they gave up on my patch. It seems like my life is a big game for them."

I was completely caught off guard with how candid and genuine he was being. I almost didn't know how to respond. "Listen man, let me see what I can do."

"What the hell do you think *YOU* can do?! You're even lower in the club than *I* am!" he interrupted. There's the attitude I'd grown accustomed to.

"Dude, just because I have a new vest doesn't mean I'm new to the club. I've been around some of these guys my whole life. I'm not saying I can make anything change, but I can see if I can pull a couple strings with some of the brothers. I'm telling you, if some of the old timers ease up on you, then the newer guys will follow their lead. I'm not saying everybody will, but some is better than none, right?"

"What do you care?" he inquired. "Because you're screwing my sister? You think using me will help make you look good?"

"No, because I can relate," I fired back. "I know what it's like to not have anybody that gives a shit about you. And I can appreciate your effort to stay clean… especially with these guys throwing it in your face every chance they get."

"What do you know about being alone?" he asked. He was still doing his best to act hard, but I could tell he was softening up toward me just a little.

"My dad devoted his life to his bike, his lifestyle, and this club while I sat at home and raised myself. My mom split before I was old enough to have memories, again leaving me to fend for myself. See a trend yet?" I answered with a healthy dose of sarcasm mixed in. I was almost offended that he thought nobody else could have a hard life, but I also knew that he didn't know my story. And just like that, the conversation sobered me up. "It never hurts to have somebody watching your back."

"Listen, you gotta be careful making those deliveries," he stated out of left field. "Do you have any idea what they're throwing you into?"

"Oh, I have a pretty good guess."

"You better have your head on a swivel," he continued. "You have to stay focused on the task at hand, but you also gotta be aware of everything around you. The guys you'll be meeting are very serious and intense. They'll try to test you to see what you're made of and if they can take advantage of you, they will. Whatever happens, you better not fail. Whatever happens at the meeting will be nothing compared to what happens if you let down the Kings."

"Sounds like you have quite a bit of experience with this," I stated.

"I've made a few runs over the last couple years. For your sake, for my *sister's* sake, just take my advice." With that, he stood up from the stool at the island and walked toward the door. "By the way," he began, pleadingly, "call me Scott."

Once he was out the door, I knew I needed to head back to my place and start writing up my next report with the latest happenings. First, I walked back to Kayla's bedroom to make sure I hadn't left anything behind in my rush earlier. I bent down to grab a pack of gum that had fallen out of my pocket when I glimpsed a photo album underneath the edge of her modest, full-size bed. I slid the album out and sat on the edge of her mattress, flipping through the pages. The book started with pictures of her parents, then pictures of her as a baby with her parents, then the photos started including Scott. It was a timeline of their family. The last page was an article cut from the local newspaper the day after her parents were killed.

Recognizing the photo album for the memorium that it was, it was as if something hit me right in the chest…or maybe it was my heart exploding from the amount of cocaine coursing through my bloodstream. I could feel my heart tighten and the beginnings of a tear in the corner of my eye. Just then, it sank in that I was toying with the lives of very real people. My mission was to bring justice to a group of outlaws, but in the process there were bound to be some innocent bystanders. I hated the thought of living a lie to a woman that I was really starting to care about, and the idea that the only family that she has left could be taken away by my actions nearly crushed me. Even though her brother had distanced himself from his former lifestyle, he was still involved with the club and undoubtedly had committed some dubious acts in the club's name. I already had first-hand information that he had transported drugs and sold large quantities, making him just as guilty as any other patched brother.

Suddenly, I felt a migraine coming on. I slipped the album back where I found it and slowly walked down to my bike. I thoughtlessly fired it up and rode to my apartment in a daze, already trying to formulate a plan to keep Scott out of this.

Chapter 14

Dear diary, (Just kidding, like I would start an official report to the DEA like that.)

Begin intelligence report: In addition to the latest occurrence of becoming an official prospect, this writer has also been approached by multiple members of the Kings of Chaos Motorcycle Club regarding the use, and possible sale, of cocaine. A patched member, road name Stitch (real name unknown), was responsible for bringing powder cocaine into this writer's apartment, and following a brief conversation with him this writer was approached by the President, Riot (real name Riot Richards), Vice President, RJ (real name Robert Johnson), and Sergeant at Arms, Mack (real name Maclin McGillicutty), to deliver a package believed to contain cocaine in exchange for another package believed to be payment at an undisclosed location and time in the future.

A GPS tracking device will be attached to this writer's motorcycle and activated when further details are received. There will be no more progress reports in the meantime, until this writer has returned from the exchange.

End of report

Short and sweet. Since I had just finished a status report a couple days ago, I didn't have a lot to add. I was sure to conveniently leave out the information involving Scott. Until I've had more time to figure something out, I don't even want to mention his name in any of my reports.

When I was confident the coast was clear, I strolled out to my motorcycle. Positive that Stitch wasn't around due to the absence of his bike, I quickly reached down to the tubing of my frame and strapped a GPS tracking unit to the bottom of my bike, out of sight from any casual observers. The unit itself was tiny with an even smaller ON/OFF switch that I could deactivate in case anybody's paranoia got the best of them and they decided to sweep my bike for electronics.

Once I finished with that small piece of business, I secured the intel in the saddlebag on the opposite side of my bike from the stacked exhaust pipes. You can never be too safe, and I didn't want the heat affecting the flash drive or the data it contained. Then I hopped in the saddle and fired it up.

Only just then, when I pulled into the parking space next to the bathroom at the Gas N' Go did it sink in how peculiar this scene might look. Why would a biker ever pull up next to a trash can and throw away a plastic bag full of trash? I couldn't think of a reasonable scenario where trash would be stowed on a bike. It's not like I would've held onto a wrapper from a snack that I might've eaten while traveling. Nope, I really didn't think this drop through at all. Regardless, I tossed the unmarked, padded envelope containing the flash drive concealed in a plastic grocery bag into the trash can and casually glanced around on my way into the restroom to see if anybody was paying attention.

Luckily, I don't think I aroused any suspicion. Also in my favor for the first time since I started this mission, I didn't bump into any other club members while making the drop. Score!

After taking a deep sigh of relief from my first drop with no run-ins, I decided to make a quick stop into the tavern. I didn't want to run the risk of being in the middle of a shift when the time came for me to take off. Not that I really cared much about losing the menial part-time job, but leaving a bar in the middle of an evening shift with no bartender would be a pretty jerk move and I don't care for the idea of screwing over the owner and other people that work there. So I strolled over to the guy that runs the joint and let him know that I would be unavailable for the next few days until I could return to work without affecting the business. Of course he had some questions that he would've liked to have answered about my impending absence, but we don't always get what we want now, do we? He's been around the block long enough to know not to get too nosey. Whether out of respect or fear, only he knows which.

Before I left the bar I made sure to catch up with Kayla for a few minutes when business was slow. It was mid-afternoon, so there weren't many patrons left from lunch and it was still a little early for the dinner rush. We just grabbed one of the smaller tables in the corner and I sipped on a glass of sweet tea while we flirted with each other. Well, my intent was to flirt a little, but apparently she had other ideas.

Without me realizing it, she had slipped off her shoe and was running her foot up the inside of my leg, all the while feigning interest in whatever I was telling her...acting like she wasn't up to anything. I played along and kept blabbing about whatever it was that I was blabbing about. Eventually, I couldn't ignore her actions anymore and was forced to acknowledge her teasing. She tilted her head back and laughed, but she didn't let that deter her from continuing her mission of making me squirm. Luckily, or not, she was forced to knock it off when a new table of customers walked in. After she left the table, I was forced to just sit there and wait until I could start thinking with the head on my shoulders before I was comfortable enough to stand up and walk through the dining area of the tavern.

Chapter 15

Wouldn't you know it, as I pulled into the parking space in front of my apartment, Mack was already waiting on me, lying back on his bike with his feet resting on top of his handlebars. Once he heard the rumble of my exhaust approach, he swung his feet down to the ground and sat up. When I pulled in next to him, he reached down behind the other side of his motorcycle and pulled up a plain black backpack.

"Here. You know the deal," the enforcer flatly said as he handed the bag to me. The only identifiable feature on the bag was a padlock, keeping the zippers from being separated to prevent the bag from being easily opened. Mack must've noticed me eye-balling the lock. "Just in case you get nosey. This will help you get where you're going," he continued, handing me a GPS unit attached to a suction cup so I could fix it to my gas tank. "It has your destination pre-programmed. Don't take any detours, and don't waste any time. Get this done and get back here if you want that patch."

"Sure thing, Mack. Just let me take a quick piss before I hit the road." I was hoping to write down the address on the other end of the GPS before I took off.

"I'll wait here with the gear," Mack responded. Well crap, there goes that idea. Oh well, it's still not a bad idea to drain my bladder before I head off on a ride that'll take me who knows where or last how long.

When I returned outside, Mack had already popped the GPS unit on my gas tank. "Junky made this run in 4 hours. Since this is your first time, you get 5. Meet us back at the clubhouse...we'll be waiting."

I simply nodded before throwing my leg over the saddle and sliding into the seat. I turned on the GPS unit so it could load, then I flipped the ignition and my bike roared to life. I slid my vest off, then reached back and stowed it in the saddlebag – any association with my actions would be very bad for club business. To protect my own identity a little bit, I popped on a shaded, full-face helmet.

Mack sat somewhat patiently on his bike, waiting for me to leave so he could start the clock. I checked the screen on the GPS, then kicked the gear lever down into first gear and rolled off.

It didn't take long before I found myself cruising southbound along US-79. I twisted the throttle and let the speedometer settle in around 75 miles per hour before engaging the throttle lock, which is a very crude form of cruise control for motorcycles. With my speed locked in, I leaned back and got as comfortable as I could for the next 100 miles.

I roared across the border on my way into Tennessee when my activity suddenly became federal business, ramping up the severity of this whole situation. I was greeted by a rather friendly sign claiming that the volunteer state welcomed me…good ol' southern hospitality at its finest. With my gas tank getting low, I decided to pull off and fill it up so my bike would be ready to go in case I had to leave with a quickness. "Always be prepared" – boy scouts 101.

According to the last road sign I passed I only had 15 miles to Clarksville. According to my GPS though, I only had 8 miles to my destination. While I was stopped at the gas station I decided to go ahead and drain my bladder again. Bumping down the highway takes its toll on you after a couple hours, plus it's nice to walk around and stretch your legs a little. Since I had a free second while my bike filled up, I reached down to the bottom of the frame and flipped the switch on the GPS tracking unit to the "on" position. When I mounted back up, I noticed more tension in my muscles and my mind wasn't near as relaxed as I had been when I was just mindlessly cruising down the pavement.

Back on the road, I switched over to US-24 West for a brief minute before exiting and making a couple turns on tiny, barely-paved back roads. Before long, I found myself tentatively entering a heavily wooded trailer park down the road from an RV park and campground. I noticed the grips were starting to feel slippery from the sweat breaking out in my palms due to nerves. My mind was racing.

I checked the GPS and realized my destination was within shouting distance. I killed my bike and walked it to the side of the drive, thinking it might be smart to be a little quieter so I could get a better feel of my surroundings before everyone knows I'm here. According to the GPS, all I had to do was walk around a small bend in the drive, and it'd be the 3rd trailer on the right. Here we go…let's do this.

I slinked along the left side of the drive to provide a little extra distance until I had a better chance to scope out point B of my journey. First thing I noticed after finding a tree stump to kneel behind was a slew of lifted pick-up trucks with tires as tall as my waist and a rust bucket of a Mustang. 1973 by my guess – not a terrible year for the pony car. There was a guy standing along the edge of the small wooden patio, smoking a cigarette. Several lights were on inside the trailer. I decided it best to wait until Captain Lung Cancer went inside before I approached.

Once the coast was clear, I cautiously stepped out from behind my hiding spot and tentatively stepped toward the trailer. Quietly padding up to the not-so-mobile home I leaned against the metal siding and listened in the best I could to the goings-on inside.

"Should be here anytime now, I figure." – Male #1.

"Let's just make sure we're ready," came the voice of a second male.

Without giving them any extra time to "get ready," whatever that meant, I stepped in front of the door and knocked solidly on the flimsy wooden plank. Captain Lung Cancer answered the door, giving me a curious stare.

"I'm here for Dirty Mike," I said as confidently as I could. Last thing I wanted was for them to pick up on any hesitance on my part.

"It's just Mike, asshole," came a reply from inside. A second later, Male #1 stepped out from behind the Captain. "Who are you?"

"Santa Claus. Looks like you've been naughty, but I have a package for you anyway. And I believe you have one for me," I stated instead of asked in order to try to keep an upper hand on the situation.

The Captain looked at Mike, who jerked his head in the direction of another backpack setting on a small dining room table. Not coincidentally, it was identical to the one on my back, down to the same style padlock connecting the zippers. The Captain handed the bag to Mike, who assured me it was all ready to go. I took him at his word, assuming he knew full well what would happen if he tried to get one over on the MC. I dropped my bag off my shoulders and laid it on the floor just inside the door. Mike tossed the bag to me while Captain Lung Cancer was walking toward my bag.

When I reached out to snag the second bag from the air, the Captain lunged at me with a stiff right jab. The force of the punch and the combination of being caught completely off guard rocked me back on my heels, and my momentum carried me down the front steps. Awkwardly, I tripped during my clumsy stumble and landed flat on my back on the ground. The Captain and Mike were both quickly coming at me. Luckily I hadn't dropped the second bag. I got back to my feet as quick as I could, shoved the Captain into Mike, slung the backpack around my arms, and ran like Hell. "Get off me! Get the car!" was all I heard while my heels were slinging dirt.

I practically leapt onto my bike the instant I was close enough and fired it up with the flick of a switch. Thank God for that electric ignition I installed! I slammed the throttle and sent the rear wheel into a slide to get the bike pointed in the opposite direction. I probably should've thought about that in the first place and had my bike ready to go. No use beating myself up over it now; you live (hopefully) and you learn. Besides, if I didn't get out of here immediately, there were a couple of other guys more than willing to deliver a beating if they had the chance.

A couple quick turns put me at the bottom of the on-ramp for US-24 East. With their headlights blinding me in my mirrors, I gunned the engine and raced onto the interstate. With the low weight of my motorcycle and the hefty motor, I felt pretty confident that I could leave them in my dust once there were no more turns or the threat of cross-traffic to deal with. Boy was I wrong.

By the time I merged onto the interstate from the on-ramp, the Mustang's headlights were growing rapidly in my mirrors. Before I knew it, the beaten and abused old muscle car was stalking my rear fender. That's when my memory decided to sucker punch me right in the gut. In 1973, the Mustang Mach I came with an optional 429 Super Cobra Jet. Just because they let the body of this beast go to Hell cosmetically doesn't mean they've neglected the heart of the stallion. I couldn't shake them, so I did my best to block them and keep them from getting beside me.

I finally got a long-overdue break when I spotted the road sign for the US-79 exit hanging above the interstate with a ½ mile warning. I stayed in front of the Mustang as long as I could with my exit coming up quick - I didn't want to telegraph my next move. At the last second I veered off across the right lane and through the cross-painted shoulder. I barely heard the sound of screeching breaks over the roar of my engine. There was no way I was letting off the throttle at least until I crossed the border.

Chapter 16

I cruised into the same truck stop on the Tennessee side of the border that I filled up at earlier. I nearly fell over when my bike came to a rest. Not because I forgot to put my feet down, but because I was shaking so badly that I had almost no strength in my limbs what-so-ever. I quickly topped off my tank to assure that I'd make it home without having to stop again, then reached down to the bottom of my frame and switched off the GPS tracking unit I had attached just hours earlier. Hopefully that little thing had just recorded my route. I'm sure the DEA wouldn't mind having that information. The adrenaline dump from the chase was really making me have to pee, but I wasn't about to take that amount of time to delay getting back on the road while I was still so close to the action. Plus, I think a little leaked out when the Mustang's front bumper was practically rubbing against my back tire, so that should've cleared out a little space in my bladder to help ensure I could make it back.

Three and a half hours after I left I pulled onto Clubhouse Road and dropped my kickstand in front of the Kings' humble abode. I speed-walked through the clubhouse, taking a quick note that the usual suspects were sitting around the table in the official meeting room, presumably waiting on my arrival. I tossed the backpack onto the table and continued to the back hallway where the bathroom was. "Be right back, gotta take a massive piss," I informed them all without waiting for a response. My gut felt like it was about to burst. I had to go so bad my eyes were floating. By the time I finished, I felt dehydrated. My midsection was cramping so bad from the rapid release I could barely stand straight.

I made my way back to the table where the guys indeed were waiting on me. When I walked in, Riot had me pull the doors closed behind me. I glanced around, first to Stitch who was too flaky to make eye contact, then to RJ who was doing an unmistakable impression of a rock, then I finally settled on Mack and Riot. Riot displayed a genuine look of admiration. Mack couldn't care less.

"Three and a half hours," Riot finally said. "Best time I've ever seen. How'd Dirty Mike treat you?"

"You could've told me not to call him Dirty Mike to his face," I offered. "Him and his little sidekick tried to make a move on me. Tried to take advantage of the situation, probably thinking they could get over on the new guy."

Riot tried his best to laugh it off like that's the same joke they pull on every new guy making a drop, but I noticed an ever-so-slight shift in his facial expression that underlied his casual response. "What'd they try pulling on you?" he asked, acting as non-interested as he could muster.

"First they tried kicking my ass and keeping both bags, but when I made it to my bike they decided that running me down would serve them just as well."

Riot couldn't ignore what I'd just told him. He knew they weren't just "picking on the new guy." Mack gave him a telling look, like this may have been a growing problem. RJ and Stitch didn't have any info to worry them, so they just sat at the table and watched the conversation unfold.

"Good job Prospect. Way to keep your wits about you and handle the situation," came the adulation from Riot.

"Prospect??" was my surprised response, remembering the deal they offered when I was assigned the task.

"Yeah. Prospect. Isn't that what the back of your cut indicates?" Riot shot back, quickly shooting me down and putting me in my place. "Now get out. Go let the guys know it's time for a meeting."

"Sure thing," was my best response right now. I've handled everything like a champ up to this point. I can't get ahead of myself and risk everything I've done to get here so far by pouting and moping around.

It was Thursday evening, so all the members were already at the clubhouse, kicking off another early start to the weekend. I made my way throughout the main room and outside to let them know they were being summoned. While the meeting took place behind closed doors as usual, I wandered around the bar area, cleaning up the empties, wiping down the bar top, and making sure the fridge was stocked. Until I got that next patch, I was still left out in the cold about club business. As I cleaned to try to keep my mind occupied, Scott sat on a barstool at the far end of the bar from the meeting room.

"Got back pretty quick," he mused. "No troubles?"

"I wouldn't say that. They tried to pull a fast one on me, but I managed to handle what they threw at me." I still thought it best not to be too forthcoming with details since it was official club business, even though I was talking to another prospect. Better safe than sorry, you know?

"PROSPECT!" came the beckon from Mack. Neither Scott nor I noticed that the left door to the meeting room had opened up, leaving most of the skull portion of the Skull King logo on the right door visible. With Mack standing alongside it in the open side of the double door, it really painted an eerie, fore-telling picture. Scott almost fell off his stool from the shock of Mack's interruption, then quickly scurried toward the big enforcer. "Not you," he simply said to Scott before turning his gaze to me. "You."

I'm not real sure how I got in the room because I really don't remember walking in, but I now found myself standing in front of a full table of patched brothers. Mack closed the door behind me. A prospect in a full meeting room? This was unsettling. I tried to be as calm, cool, and collected as possible waiting for a hint of what was going on. I had a hope, but until something was offered by an officer I had no clue what to expect.

Then I saw it; the Skull King patch sitting front and center in the middle of the table. "We gave you our word, and the one thing this club doesn't do to brothers is lie to them. If you pick up that patch, you better be ready and willing to live up to that."

All I could do was nod my head.

Riot continued, "Me and your old man might not've seen eye to eye when I was coming up, but there was never a question about his loyalty to this club. I'll admit it, my hard feelings toward your dad kept me from liking you a whole lot, but these other guys told me to give you a shot. It seems like they were right. Understand what taking that patch means. You better think long and hard to make sure you grasp that."

Without hesitation I reached out for the table and snatched up the patch. My patch. I was forced to acknowledge the lump in my throat. Was I really this excited? The realization of being one step closer to completing my mission made me stand a bit straighter. The realization of being one step closer to betraying a group of outlaws made it hard to breathe.

"Let's vote," said Riot. "All in favor of our first legacy patched brother, say aye." A unanimous group response followed. "There we have it. Legacy it is." Everybody at the table started clapping, whistling, and yelling. I was in. Every member stood and approached me with a hug, handshake, fist bump, high five, or any combination of those.

After the excitement of the vote settled down, Riot moved on to the next piece of business. "Pull up a chair, Legacy," he directed me. I wasn't accustomed to being included in this part, so the idea to have a seat hadn't occurred to me. "After our new brother returned from his run this afternoon, he informed us of some shenanigans during the exchange. We're all well aware that Dirty Mike and his boys are half inbred and all idiot, but if Legacy's testament is true then they may have just crossed the line between friendly play with a newbie and trying to take advantage of

86

us. RJ heard the story and I'd like to hear his thoughts."

"Well," RJ began deliberately. "Sounds like Dirty Mike got a little greedy and tried to send Will back empty handed. Will – err, Legacy, handled himself like we would expect any of our members to and managed to get back with what is rightfully ours. BUT, only after nearly getting run down on the highway. This wasn't some innocent little prank on the new guy. This was a legitimate threat from some backwoods dirtbag. Now we have to decide how to handle it."

The old timers weren't too thrilled to hear about the events of my run and nearly losing a prospect that they share a lot of history with and so they showed a fair amount of outrage and concern. Riot banged his gavel down on the table to remind the brothers that there were official proceedings at hand.

Riot progressed, "I suggest a few of us ride down there. Have a little impromptu meeting with ol' Dirty and see what he has to say for himself. Myself, Mack, and Legacy will meet face-to-face with him and see what the story was through his eyes. RJ and Griz, you'll hang back out of sight in case things escalate. I don't intend to blow this thing up, but if he doesn't recognize the problem then I am damn sure going to squash any plans he might be thinking about. All in favor..."

"Aye," came the unanimous decision from the brothers.

"Let's drink!" Riot concluded as he banged his gavel one more time to dismiss the meeting.

I happened to be closest to the doors, so I spun around and opened them both, unintentionally in a rather grand manner.

"PROSPET!" Mack yelled from behind me. "Get over here and congratulate our newest brother."

Scott cocked his head slightly, somewhat confused about what was being said. He did as he was told and started walking toward the meeting room when I held up my patch for him to see. He congratulated and hugged me, but I could see a flicker of anger and jealousy flash behind his eyes.

"There's a sewing machine in the back closet, across from my room," he offered through gritted teeth. There was no hesitation when a brother was voted in to get the patch prominently displayed as soon as possible.

The party started with a couple of the guys trying to forcefully remove my colors. Just because I was officially a full-patch brother now didn't mean that I didn't still have to prove my worth. A biker will protect his colors with his life, and while I knew it wouldn't come to that right then, I still had to make sure my patch stayed on my back.

The night ended with beer and liquor flowing freely, and me crashing on a couch in the front room.

Chapter 17

I awoke from RJ kicking the bottom of my boot. "Wake up," he said. "Go home and get cleaned up. Riot wants to leave by 5."

"What time is it now?" was my groggy response.

"Almost 2. Last night was a pretty good time huh?"

I nodded very slowly to keep the vomit in my stomach where it belonged.

"Well, the fun and games are done. Today is business. Be back here no later than 5 so we can ride out. Gotta get this business with Dirty Mike handled. And wash your damn face."

I slowly sat up and hung my head in my hands for a few minutes until the floor stopped spinning and leveled out. After what seemed like forever, I made my way to my feet and shuffled outside to my bike. I dropped down on the kickstarter and wasn't sure if it were me or the bike that fell over. All I could tell is that things were at angles that they normally weren't. I laid on the ground for a few minutes to compose myself before climbing back up and dusting myself off. I jumped on the ol' kickstarter again, landed on my feet, and brought the beast to life. "Ugh. So. Loud," I thought to myself. If I was going to make it through the rest of this day, I needed hydration and lots of it. I climbed onto the bike and checked my mirrors before I set off toward my apartment. That's when I saw what RJ meant about needing to wash my face. Evidently, after I passed out on the couch, the guys thought it would be hilarious to draw phalluses all over my face. That's a nice word for wieners. I had multiple wieners drawn on my face.

A couple minutes later I pulled into the parking lot and there was Stitch laying against the front door of his apartment again. I walked by and kicked his boot. "Come on, man."

He struggled to come back to life much as I had about twenty minutes prior.

He stumbled to his feet with a few grunts and groans thrown in for good measure.

The little boy was running around outside in nothing more than a diaper. "Does that boy have any actual clothes?" I asked, thumbing in the direction of the child.

"I don't know. It ain't my kid," came his response.

My blood boiled at his lack of responsibility. Eventually, Stitch found his way through my front door and to my couch. No other words needed exchanged. I stepped toward my apartment when the door next to mine cracked open and my neighbor started yelling for the child to go inside. Apparently, his only supervision had been an unconscious Stitch, and now that his presence was gone, the mother of the year decided it was time for the boy to return home. You're doing a great job, lady.

As Stitch passed out on my couch, I made my way to the kitchen to get the biggest pitcher I could find to fill with water, then downed about a third of it before coming up for air. The pitcher and I then sloshed our way back to my bedroom. I pushed the door closed without latching it so I could listen for any movement that may come from my living room before logging onto my computer. I started and finished a progress report in less time than it took to drink my pitcher of water.

Begin intelligence report: I'm in. Drugs run through Clarksville, TN. Will have more intel by end of this week.

End of report

Because there is a lag in the delivery system, telling the DEA of the meeting today would be irrelevant. By the time they knew about it, it would be handled. Just another obstacle keeping this mission from running efficiently; government work at its finest. I couldn't just send an email to my supervisor at the agency; not with Stitch running into my apartment whenever his old lady didn't feel like unlocking the door for him. I don't have any illusions that Stich is capable of developing theories and running a little investigation of his own, but you can't be too careful in my situation. The second you underestimate somebody is the second your cover is blown and quite possibly even worse than that…much worse.

Before I left, I stepped into my bathroom and grabbed a washcloth to erase the primitive cave drawings that were defacing my money-maker. Of course they had used permanent markers and ink pens, so I was basically forced to scrub my epidermis off like the washcloth was made out of sandpaper.

I swung through the Gas N' Go, topped off my tank and made the drop in the trash can by the bathroom. Now it's up to the agency's guy that works for the county waste management company to pull that bag and deliver it to the DEA for sorting. Then it's up to the DEA to sift through and make sure they don't discard my package.

From there I felt the desire to make a stop at the tavern. I walked in and grabbed a small table in the corner, as far away from the sun-filled windows as possible. The owner caught my eye and made his way to my table.

"Hey Will," he began. "Any thoughts on your availability in the near-future? I can't have you taking time off because you're unavailable, just to have you end up coming in here to eat. Kinda pisses off the other bartenders, ya know?"

I just listened.

"And what's this mess I hear about going on with Randy a few nights ago? Listen, you start wearing a vest, then my patrons start getting in fistfights. That's not a coincidence I'm willing to ignore. These little 'outbursts' can't continue. Are we on the same page?"

"Who the hell is Randy??" was my retort, even though I knew it's the guy that has a little less tongue now than he did a week ago. "I hear you. Don't worry, I'm not trying to take over your bar and neither is the club. I had just gotten my vest that night and was feeling a little superior. It was a very minor incident that lasted less than 2 minutes. Look on the bright side, with me wearing this vest, your place will be well looked after as long as I'm around."

"Minor incident?! The guy has a lisp so bad now, he sounds like Paul Stanley anytime he pronounces an 'S'! And are you insinuating that my business won't be so safe if you aren't around??"

He read between the lines a little more than I intended for, but no reason to back down. I stood and simply dipped my head. Before I walked away, I finished the conversation. "I'll be back at work Monday." I'm sure the Skull King patch on my back taunted him the entire time I walked out of the tavern.

I stepped out of the bar and into the stairwell leading up to Kayla's place. I reached the top of the stairs and started knocking on the door three times. It opened mid-knock on number three and there stood Kayla with a smile in her eyes. I walked in and gave her a long hard kiss just inside the threshold of the doorway. As we pulled apart, she sauntered into the kitchen and poured herself a glass of milk. It does a body good, ya know? It's done *her* body good, that's for sure!

"Scott told me about you taking over for him as the new prospect," she started in. "I knew you said you could make a difference for him, but I didn't think it would be so quick."

"Slow down, Kayla," I cut in. "I told you I would see what I could do and I did manage to take some pressure off of him since I've been wearing this vest."

"But…" she sensed it coming.

"But." I slid my vest off of my back and spun it around so she could see the back of it fully adorned. "It seems he has no choice but to retain his position as their prospect." I could see her heart crumble as her eyes welled up a little. "The good news is I should have more influence as a full patch member. Hopefully I can intervene and get some of the guys off his back a little."

"Yeah. Maybe," came her response. It didn't take a behavioral scientist to notice the sudden change in her demeanor.

I took the hint, and started making my way toward the door. "Anyway, I have to make a run with some of the guys tonight. Just wanted to stop in and see you. I won't forget about my promise to you and Scott, I assure you. Oh yeah, I'll be back at work on Monday." I leaned in and gave her a quick kiss on the cheek and I left it at that. Time to get back to the clubhouse.

Chapter 18

I pushed open the front door of the clubhouse and saw Griz sitting at the bar with a couple of empties in front of him and another not-so empty that his right hand was wrapped around. "Nothing like a little hair of the dog, eh?" he asked as he raised a bottle and took a swig.

"Nothing like still being drunk right before a ride," I chided him.

"Whoa, who invited the police?" he shot back.

He was right. Definitely not the right approach with these guys.

"Just us so far?" I asked. He confirmed by holding out his arm and presenting the empty room that we were occupying. "Right. Dumb question." Drunk Griz is kind of a buzzkill.

Right then, we caught the sound of an approaching bike or two. I peeked out the window and saw Riot and Mack pull up to the front of the house. As they were walking toward the door, I saw RJ turn onto Clubhouse Road and approach the house. Minutes later, we were all gathered in the front room.

Riot spoke up and naturally took control. "Alright, pretty simple gameplan. We ride down, me, Mack, and Legacy ask Dirty Mike what he was thinking, make our displeasure clear, then we ride back. We leave it at that. If Mike has other ideas, then RJ and Griz won't be far away as our support. This doesn't have to change any arrangements that are already in place, but we also have to be prepared for the worst. If things go south, then our business strategy will have to be adjusted. We'll deal with that when the time comes if we need to. Questions?" We all shook our heads. Griz hiccupped. "Let's ride. We'll stop on the way out of town to top off our tanks."

Before long we were riding down Route 79 in a staggered formation. Even outlaws have codes they live by. Riding in a pack in an organized fashion is one of those guidelines. Staggering the position of the bikes offers the most safety in case of bad fortune. If somebody were to happen to go down for some reason, it gives the rest of the riders an escape route from harm's way. If everybody was riding single file and a rider goes down, then the rest of the line just piles on top of him and that's all she wrote. With the staggered formation, half of the riders should be in the clear in the event of a mishap, and the bikes behind the downed rider should be spread out enough to give them ample response time to adjust accordingly to avoid disaster. The President rides front left, leading his club as always. To the right, but just behind the lead bike is the VP. With such a small group, the rest of us just fell in line with me bringing up the rear since I was the new guy.

As we rode past the state line road sign, I swung out and passed the others before merging back in front of them. About a mile down the road I led them down the off-ramp to the gas station I stopped at yesterday. We congregated around a couple pumps to refill our tanks and stretch our legs. Riot and Mack walked into the truck stop to empty their bladders while Griz and I topped off our tanks.

"Good find on the truck stop, Rookie," Griz started in. Somehow, it seemed his words were more slurred now than they were before we left Rough River Falls. I guess riding out in the sun caused a little more dehydration, prolonging his buzz. But hey, what do I know? I'm no doctor.

Just then, Griz pulled the gas pump out of his tank without relaxing his grip on the handle and sprayed gasoline all over the tank of his bike. "Son of a-!" he blurted as he witnessed the reality of his drunkenness. I doubled over in laughter, kneeling down to one knee because my legs nearly buckled from the outburst. RJ, who had been standing next to me, leaned on me for support so we each didn't have to pick ourselves off the ground.

"Smooth, Griz. Dumbass…" came Riot's response as he and Mack exited the gas station. He couldn't hide the grin on his face. A small smile even crossed Mack's lips for a brief (very brief) moment.

Griz's whole head, from the tip of his nose to the back of his neck, turned beet red from his gaffe as embarrassment sank in. As the situation played out some more, it ended with a quick squirt from Griz, holding the pump like a water gun. The gas station employee poked his head out through the door.

"Hey! That's gasoline, you idiots!" he ridiculed.

The realization of the safety hazard finally struck Griz and he decided to hang up the pump.

"Alright numb-nuts, let's get going," came the instruction from Riot.

We all mounted up and tore out of the gas station to get back on track. Once we got back on the highway we re-established formation. Quickly, it was time to make our turn onto US-24, followed by the same turns onto the barely there paved backroads of Tennessee. We passed the RV park and RJ and Griz began to slow down and separate from our group. Riot, Mack and I entered the trailer park and drove straight up to ol' Dirty's place. No sense in sneaking up on them this time I figured. I highly doubt they were expecting a second visit in as many days.

As we climbed off our bikes, the front door swung open and Mike filled the opening, leaning against the door frame. "Looky here, it's the new guy," he said with a smirk.

"Cut the shit. You don't talk to him when I'm standing right here," Riot interjected, cutting off the unnecessary posturing. "Address me and only me when I'm in front of you." Riot meant business. This could get real interesting real fast.

"What's with the 'big, bad biker' routine? Who pissed in your gas tank?" Mike shot back. You could see the displeasure on his face with how this confrontation was beginning.

"My guy here tells me you might have had some different ideas on how our interactions need to go down," Riot stated, nodding his head in my direction.

Mike's eyes trailed over to me and the sleazy smirk returned. "Not sure what you're talking about. Maybe you should ask my guy about getting thrown down these very steps. I think maybe 'your guy' didn't give you the whole story." He paused a second for effect. "We were here, waiting for the bag as usual. Your boy over there comes knocking, calling us all mean and hurtful names, shoves my guy down the stairs and tries to take off with both bags. We chased him down in the car before he finally gave up and dumped one of the bags. That's how I remember it. Sound about right to you, Jimmy?" he shouted back inside the trailer. "Yep, nailed it," came a response from inside.

"Well then, seems to be some conflicting stories that we've been presented with," Riot began. "The only thing that really bothers me, is that this isn't the first time we've heard about your bullshit shenanigans." Riot's tone was calm, but his words were the exact opposite.

I felt a chill travel from the base of my neck all the way down my spine. For as "cordial" as this conversation had been so far, there was an undeniable tension weighing down like an anvil.

The second male from inside the trailer appeared behind Mike. Mack took a step closer from behind Riot and I. Just then, a muffled sound came from behind us. I could tell it was from across the street, and I instantly knew it was related to Griz. I received confirmation as I turned my head just enough to see Griz stumbling over the tree stump that I had hidden behind yesterday.

"What is this?!" demanded Mike, as he pulled a pistol and trained it on Riot's chest.

Mack drew a gun of his own and aimed for center mass of Dirty Mike.

As calm as he had been the whole time, Riot looked at Mike. "Put that gun down or Mack will put you down. Make up your mind quick though, because Mack isn't known for his patience."

The standoff continued longer than I expected it to, but Mike eventually began lowering his gun. As his arm reached his side, Jimmy sprang from behind Mike. He lunged from the door toward the first person he could reach, but before he could get to his destination a shot rang out, shattering the dark, quiet, country night. Jimmy fell to the ground limp and lifeless. Blood blossomed out of his back from the exit wound.

Riot drew on Mike, who stood in the doorway in shock. His jaw was slack and he wasn't sure how to respond to this situation. Riot addressed him as composed as ever. "Mike, this is on you. You screw around with our business and this is what happens. This partnership will continue whether you want it to or not. Nothing like this will ever happen again as long as you remember your role. Your next decision could be the most important of your life. You stand there and we'll get on our bikes and leave, our partnership intact. Then you can clean up Jimmy here afterward. OR…you make a move and end up lying right next to him. Either way, it's way past time for us to be going." He glanced at Mack, silently letting him know to keep his gun pointed in Mike's direction while Riot climbed on his bike. As Riot strolled past me, he simply instructed, "Let's go."

Once Riot and I were on our bikes, we kept our eyes on Mike while Mack mounted his motorcycle. We needed to get out of here, quickly, but we couldn't let our guard down after what had just happened. We fired up our bikes and walked them back to get our front ends pointed away from the trailer. I really need to remember to think ahead and park this thing pointed in the right direction. Almost simultaneously, we all stomped on the shift lever and dropped the bikes into first gear. Even more synchronized, we all ripped open the throttles and tore out of the trailer park, RJ and Griz joining us on the way out.

Our engines screamed as we approached the highway. I kept checking my mirror, waiting to see the all-too-familiar headlights of the Mustang, but they never appeared. My heart was racing. Without a doubt, my beats per minute were higher than the five thousand RPM's that my tachometer was showing at the time. I just witnessed a murder. Not only that, but I had a part in it. How the hell do I write a status report where I was involved in a murder?!

My thoughts were as erratic as my heartbeat all the way back to Rough River Falls. After we pulled up to the clubhouse, Riot climbed off his bike and looked at each of us. "Go home. Take it easy for a few days. Lay low and stay quiet until I can get a pulse on this situation. Once I know more, I'll fill the rest of you in. RJ, we need to sit down together and figure out where we stand as a club."

RJ shut down his bike and he and Riot walked into the dark clubhouse. Mack, Griz, and myself glanced at each other briefly, then followed orders and rolled out.

Chapter 19

Back at my apartment, it was time to write the hardest thing I've ever had to type in my life. I could feel my heart beating out of my chest. I could feel it pulsing in my fingers, legs, and worst of all, I felt it in my splitting migraine that was no doubt caused by what I had just witnessed. Worse than witnessed – been involved in.

Very delicately, I started weaving my yarn of how events played out. I included the details from the first meeting with Mike and his groupies and how the exchange went down with the subsequent chase scene that was taken straight out of "Gone in 60 Seconds." I made sure to include how my personal safety was uncertain. That's an important little detail to include. From there, I filled in the particulars about the return visit to the trailer park. I incorporated the face-off with Riot and Dirty Mike, then kind of blurred the lines around reality a little for my own sake. I couldn't very well admit to being a front row bystander to a murder without taking responsible action and blowing my cover, so I just led them to believe that there was a small fracas, and a shot or two was fired while we made our exit. They can't hold me accountable and expect me to blow this investigation over something I'm not sure happened. Now it's up to the DEA to make contact with the Montgomery County Sheriff's Office in Tennessee and keep things quiet so my own investigation doesn't come to a grinding halt. There's no way the club would go about business as usual if they knew there was a law enforcement agency on their radar.

The weekend passed and I never left my apartment. Kayla and I exchanged a few text messages, but I let her believe that I had come down with something and didn't want to infect her with my germs. I really didn't have much interest in visitors and having to talk to somebody right now.

Monday morning rolled around and I decided to take a shower and put on clean clothes for the first time in over 2 days. After all, I was due back at the tavern for the evening shift. Attempting to act normal meant I needed to keep appearances – for the town, club, and DEA. Yep, I am now officially keeping secrets from my job, my club, and my ol' lady. That's not awesome.

I strolled into Rusty's five minutes before my shift started. I spotted Kayla across the family room to my right, and stayed on my path toward the bar. I sensed that she detected me and began working her way toward me.

"Hey there, feelin' better?" she quipped.

"Good enough, I guess," was my response. Man, it was good to see her, but I couldn't help but feel guilty. Guilty for involving her with me; for associating her with the disaster that is my life. Do I cut her loose, and hope she appreciates the sacrifice down the road sometime? Or keep dragging her down right along with me?

"Well, good to see you back out in the wild." With that, she spun around and resumed balancing 4 open beverages and 4 plates full of food on a single tray like it was no big deal. She probably could've done it on roller skates with one arm tied behind her back. Maybe I'll propose that to her sometime later on.

It was a Monday night, so the business was slow and my shift crept by at a snail's pace. I was fine with that. With my mental state, I was happier washing a sinkful of glasses as opposed to listening to some drunk whine about his insignificant personal problems. About halfway through the evening I heard the bell above the door rattle, so I glanced up and saw Scott coming my way. "What's up, man?"

"Not shit." He was so eloquent. "Things have been pretty quiet lately, so I figured I'd check in and see what was going on."

Well this could get tricky. I'm not free to discuss the events of the weekend on a club level *or* a DEA standpoint. Not to mention, Scott still isn't a full patch brother. "Not much happening. Probably why it's been so quiet." Good one, Mr.

Obvious.

"I get it. You can't talk to me. Whatever," he acknowledged. "I was just curious why the clubhouse was pretty much abandoned all weekend. I had to hang out with Stitch by myself…I guess his ol' lady got tired of his shit and kicked him out, so he's been crashing on one of the couches."

"Ugh, that guy…" I trailed off. "I feel for you man. I've never seen anybody get road rash from a couch, but that'd be the guy to make it happen." I tried to keep the conversation light and steer it away from anything substantial.

"Listen, about you getting voted in," he started. Great, so much for nothing substantial. "I'm super pissed about it, but don't get me wrong, I'm happy for you. I get that you have a lot of history with a bunch of these guys, it's just hard to see a new face around the club get voted in as a full patch member and I'm still over here mopping up puke and piss every night."

"Ah yes, the two P's," is all I could think to reply with. Brilliant. "I hear ya, Scott. I'm not crazy about how the club treats you either. Now that I have my patch, I'll see if I can't start getting these guys to ease up a little more."

"I don't need a babysitter, man. Just don't take my bullshit personal. And quit making out with my sister when I'm around." He left it at that and started walking out of the bar.

"I'm not making any promises, Prospect!" I chided him on his way through the door. I could easily make out his one-fingered salute as the door closed behind him. What can I say? That kid's growing on me.

My shift thankfully ended and I split as quickly as I could. Kayla wanted me to stick around and talk to her, but I wasn't really feeling that given all of the confusion swimming around in my head the past week, so I just went to my apartment.

I plopped down on my couch and turned the TV on as I turned my brain off.

I flipped through the channels for a few minutes before settling on some mindless soap opera about some random superhero. The next thing I knew my front door was bursting open, but I hadn't invited anybody over. "Stitch, tonight's not gonna work," I said as I turned my head toward the open door frame.

"Sorry to interrupt your plans," Came the response from Riot. He and Mack walked into my living room with a purpose.

"What's up, guys?"

"Get up." Riot instructed.

Umm, okay. As I stretched my legs and stood in front of my Prez and Sergeant at Arms, Mack threw a tremendous body blow right into my gut. I doubled over instantly, right into an uppercut from the big bruiser. The second shot sent me back up where Mack landed a massive punch to my left cheek. I went down to the floor and tried to cover up the best I could to protect myself from taking any more damage. Mack lifted his leather boot and stomped it down onto my hip, opening up my midsection for a kick from Riot.

What the hell was happening?! I've already been voted in to this club, so this couldn't be some sort of initiation. Neither of them were wearing masks, so they're trying to send a very clear message of some sort. Unfortunately, I had no clue what that message might be. It's kinda hard to think straight when your brain's been rattled by a barrage of punches and kicks and you're writhing around on the floor in pain. Had I been found out? Was there a leak somewhere that Riot had access to that told him the DEA was running point over the Montgomery County Sheriff's Office over the murder of some loser named Jimmy?

Finally, Riot spoke up. "When you jeopardize our enterprise, then there are consequences you have to pay. The only reason you're still alive is because of that patch on your back; we don't kill our own. Junky has made that run countless times and there's never been an incident that threatened our business relationships. We send you one time and somebody ends up dead over it."

So I guess this means that Riot might still have some ill-will toward me. Point taken. "Thanks?" was all I could muster. The only thing coming to my aid at that time was my sarcastic defense mechanism. What a huge help…

Riot sent another steel-toed shot right into my kidney just for good measure as he and Mack strolled out of my apartment. They didn't even close the door behind them. Assholes.

It took me awhile to gather the strength to pick myself up off the floor and stagger over to the door to close it. From there, I hobbled into the bathroom to assess the damage and get cleaned up. There was a gash above my left eye, which was already mostly swollen shut, and my cheek was pretty puffy to boot. I sat on the toilet and strained to piss. I glanced into the toilet before flushing and saw some blood droplets, slowly mixing in. As bad as it felt now, I had a strong feeling it was gonna hurt a lot worse in the morning. Call it a hunch.

Chapter 20

I was right. I woke up the next morning and wished I wouldn't have. Son of a bitch, this was going to be a long day! I couldn't see out of my left eye, my stomach was so sore it hurt to stand straight, and my hip was bruised so bad it hurt to walk. I managed to get myself together enough to get to my truck. I had to get out of there; away from that crime scene.

I found myself pulling into Rusty's parking lot. I knew Kayla wasn't working from checking the schedule while I was at the bar the previous night, so I gingerly made my way up the stairs to her front door. I started my regular routine of knocking three times, but the door flung open after the first one. I know her apartment is small, but is she some kind of magician? That's just uncanny.

"Have you seen Scott?" she asked frantically.

"Uh, hi. No." I really have to get a grip on being so confused all of the time. Is the DEA really trusting this investigation to somebody that can't start an interaction with other people on equal footing?

"I haven't heard from him since he left the tavern last night," she continued. I was trying to check on him last night to see how he's doing, because I know he's been struggling with you being patched in. Good lord, what happened to you?!" Seamless transition of topics there.

"Nothing big, just a couple unwanted guests last night." There was no way I could let anybody know what happened last night. I have to maintain my loyalty to the club if I want any chance of getting what I needed. "I talked to Scott for a few minutes last night when he stopped into the tavern."

"I know, that's why I asked if you've seen him." Well that makes sense.

"I can go check the clubhouse. He's probably just passed out or something. Maybe the guys kept him up late last night," I said, trying my best to comfort her.

"Are you sure you should be moving? You look like hell," she stated the obvious, shifting her worry from Scott to me.

"It's fine. It only hurts when I'm awake," I assured her. She gave me a very delicately placed peck before sending me on my way. Wish I would've known to go to the clubhouse first so I didn't have to waste my time with these God-forsaken stairs.

I pulled up to the front of the clubhouse and started making my way inside. There wasn't much activity, but Stitch was there shooting pool alone. I thought I heard some movement from the meeting room, so I bypassed Stitch and walked in the direction of the sound. I couldn't even be bothered to make some snarky, sarcastic comment. Yeah, I know. I peeked my head into the meeting room and saw Riot combing through the metal cabinet in the corner. He must've sensed my presence, because he started talking without looking at me.

"Didn't expect to see you today. I wasn't sure how you would react to last night's lesson," he stated dismissively.

"Is that what you're calling it? A 'lesson?'" I asked. "I thought of it more as an aggravated assault."

"Did you call the cops? If there's no police report, then it didn't happen," he succinctly pointed out.

"Well, I guess nothing happened then. Just some club business, right?" I had to make sure Riot knew there was no concern about me running out and snitching. He would find that out on his own eventually…on my terms, not his. "What are you up to, by the way?" I had to keep cool and act as normal as possible to make sure I didn't alienate myself from the people that could give me the information I was looking for.

"Just looking for something. I want to have a meeting tonight. Let the guys know," he ordered.

"Where's the prospect? Can't he do it?" I inquired.

"I've got him handled. You get the rest of the brothers." His command was delivered with resolve. It would be pointless to keep asking questions or complain about my task.

I went back into the main area of the clubhouse and finally acknowledged Stitch. "Riot wants a meeting tonight," I informed him. I plodded over to one of the couches, hopefully the one that Stitch hadn't been rubbing his filth into the past few nights, and started calling all of the brothers to let them know about the meeting.

*****

By 7:00 that evening, the meeting room was filled with full patch brothers. Nobody seemed aware of what was going on, but several of them had shown interest in knowing what had happened to me. I tried to downplay it as much as possible. "Nothing I couldn't handle," I tried to convince them. Before I had to start making up a story to explain my injuries, Riot thankfully pounded the table with his gavel.

"Alright, let's get to it," he began. "I'm sure you are all probably curious about what we're doing here tonight. Well, there's something I wanted to address and I didn't want to wait 'til Sunday."

Oh, well then there we have it. That explains everything. Nope. No it doesn't. And the curious glances around the room confirmed that it didn't help a single person know what was happening.

Riot threw a Skull King patch on the table. Wait, what? Now he had the undivided attention of every guy in the room. "I think two years is a pretty long time. Probably too long in all reality." Now there were some head nods and smiles as it was starting to sink in to some of the Kings about what was going on. "I think it's about time we take a vote on patching in Junky."

"What about his bike situation?" came a question from one of the brothers. I cocked my head to the side quizzically, not knowing what he meant by that.

"Obviously, you can't be in a motorcycle club without a bike. Leave that to me. I've got it all worked out," Riot answered with a shit-eating grin on his face. I can't say I liked the look and sound of that at all. And I guess I never really paid attention to Scott's mode of transportation, but maybe that has had something to do with him not being patched in. "All in favor..." Riot continued. This is where I got a little nervous. Prospects only get put up for a vote once, and the decision has to be unanimous. Either you're in or you're out.

Riot went around the room, one by one, starting with RJ to his left. RJ gave a nod. Riot continued to each member individually, who affirmed their vote until it ended with Mack giving his approval. So it was decided, Scott was officially a full patch brother! Riot announced it and a cheer went up around the room.

Riot calmed everyone and resumed the meeting. "Okay, so then that brings us to our next piece of business. We need to fill the vacancy we now have at our hang-around and prospect level."

"I have a suggestion," Griz spoke up. "I know a kid that might be up for what we throw at him. He's been around my shop a few times, and he always seems to be into something. I think he'd be able to handle himself. He's young though."

Surely he wasn't talking about the kid with the now deformed face, was he? That kid was more messed up than I was right now, and that was from weeks ago. I interjected. "Griz, you don't mean...?"

"Yep. The kid has guts and you and I both already know he won't be afraid to get into trouble from time to time," he replied.

"Anybody else have any other suggestions?" Riot asked. Nobody spoke up, so Riot looked directly at me. "Legacy, you seem to have some ideas on the situation. What do you think?"

I had to be careful here. With being the FNG, any decision I made regarding the club would be highly scrutinized by older members. Not only did I have to prove my worth to the club, but I also had to prove my judgement. I'd already learned about the consequences when things don't go smoothly for the club. "Griz knows better than I do. If he thinks it's a good idea, then I won't argue," I said and left it at that.

"Alright then Griz, reach out and see what his response is. One last thing, since this is your guy, you'll be sponsoring him. If he blows it, then it's on you." Griz accepted that burden and Riot concluded the meeting.

Mack flung the doors open to the meeting room and yelled for the prospect, but I still didn't see Scott anywhere. Mack beckoned again, louder this time. After a few seconds, Scott came scurrying out from the back hallway that led to his room.

"Sorry guys," he said, entering the room. "Riot told me to hang out and stay out of the way for awhile. What's up?"

Riot stepped out from behind Mack and spoke up. The other brothers fell silent in anticipation. "Junky, we've been talking and we decided that we can't have an official prospect hanging around the club without a bike. I'd say we've given you more than enough time to find your own set of wheels, yet here we are." Riot was putting on a good show and I could see every feeling that Scott was going through written plainly on his face; rejection, heart-shattering misery. This kid was being put through the ringer. "We've decided that this charade has gone on too long."

Riot approached Scott, put his arm around Scott's neck and began leading him out of the clubhouse. The brothers were just as confused about what was happening at this point as Scott was. Riot opened the front door and walked down the few steps leading to the ground with Scott in tow. Everybody else followed. "We can't have members without a ride," Riot said, holding out his arms to display a scooter parked in the front yard. "So here ya go!" The club erupted with laughter.

Scott's face turned beet red, either from embarrassment or rage. While on the surface it was a very generous gesture, in the biking community scooters are a flat-out joke. This was the most backhanded gift that Scott could have been given.

"Oh yeah, here's this too," Riot finally finished, tossing the Skull King patch into Scott's chest. Scott's expression immediately shifted gears as he fumbled to catch the patch and not let it touch the ground. "Better go get that put on before one of these guys takes it from you." With that, Scott disappeared back into the clubhouse to sew his patch onto his vest and the party was on.

Chapter 21

Music wailed from the stereo speakers and the beer flowed freer than I'd ever seen at the clubhouse while everyone celebrated our newest member. Since we were currently prospect-less, it was every man for himself when it came to refills, but nobody seemed to mind.

The party raged on for hours. I did my best to keep my distance from people so I didn't get bumped into. With my current state of affairs, any physical contact whatsoever was excruciating. I glanced around to see if I could spot Scott, to no avail. What I did notice though, was Riot and Mack making a raucous entrance into the main room from the back of the clubhouse. I excused myself from whatever pointless conversation I was currently having and limped toward the back hallway toward Scott's room. I made eye contact with Riot on my way across the room, and he flashed a mischievous smile in my direction. I doubt that can mean anything good.

Eventually, I made my way to Scott's door and proceeded with my standard three knock ritual. Nobody answered, but I heard some groaning from behind the door. I twisted the knob and slowly opened the door, expecting to see Scott being "entertained" by one of the female companions of the club. The horror of what I actually found was infinitely worse. As the door swung open, I saw Scott sitting in a chair with his back to me. I quickly realized he wasn't just sitting there, but he was strapped to the chair. I stepped around to the front of him, instantly noticing the syringe dangling from his arm. He was still conscious, but he was in bad shape. His pupils were so dilated, they almost covered his entire Iris.

"What the hell happened, Scott?" I asked aloud, not really expecting any coherent response.

His mouth opened like he was about to answer me, then immediately proceeded to puke all over himself. I jumped back as quickly as I could, trying to avoid being splattered by any debris. "Let it out," I encouraged him. The best thing he could do right now is continue to vomit. He needed to get whatever it was out of his body before his bloodstream could soak up anymore chemicals. Satisfied that this was the safest position he could be in right now, instead of laying on the floor where he could suffocate on his own chum, I marched directly back to the front room of the clubhouse and scanned it for Riot.

"What the hell did you give him?!" I demanded as soon as I located our Prez.

"Who? Junky? I gave him what he wanted...his patch," he answered. "And a celebration that he won't forget," he laughed.

More like a bad trip that he won't remember.

Riot went on, "He was having a good time and wanted to make it better, so I supplied the essentials..."

"You tied him down and shot him up, you bastard!" I spat. Without even being aware of my actions, I cocked back my right arm and sucker punched my Prez right in the lips. Everybody else stopped what they were doing immediately and gathered around.

Standard MC code dictates that you have your brother's back when it comes to fighting at all times, no matter what. A club will ratpack anybody and everybody to protect their own. But when it comes to two members from the same club fighting, then you don't interfere...even if one of the combatants is the Prez. Any beef between brothers gets settled the old fashioned way.

I managed to land some pretty good shots, and had him backpedaling. I grabbed the collar of his shirt, hockey style so he couldn't get too far away from me. He was a lot quicker than me due to my injuries, but I was determined and trained on how to fight through pain. I landed some body blows, connecting with his ribs a couple times. I think he was caught totally by surprise because he never reacted and threw any punches of his own. Once we began to slow down a little, I felt two giant fists slam down on my upper back, and I immediately hit the floor.

Mack spoke up, "That's enough. Everybody out," he ordered. Code be damned I guess when your Prez is getting his ass handed to him.

I managed to get back to my feet after several painful minutes. Riot was still right where I left him, but he was now hunched over, down on one knee trying to recoup and gather his wits. He stood, met my gaze, and simply said, "This ain't over," as he walked by me, bumping into my shoulder with purpose.

You're damn right it ain't. I wasn't about to back down again without putting up a fight of my own, even if it meant taking another beating. "Is this how you treat your 'brothers?'" I asked Riot, openly mocking the validity of the club.

"Call it job security," he retorted. "He used to be one of our best customers. We just can't let that kind of business walk away, now can we?"

"Well now that's he's a brother, he's gonna eat into your profits. Didn't really think that through, did you?"

That's where you're wrong," he said eerily calm. "It's not Junky's use that I want to secure...it's his friend's. All we have to do is keep them alive this time," he trailed off as he sauntered out of the room.

What in the blue hell was he implying?!

Chapter 22

I called Kayla from the parking lot of the tavern. After the "celebration"
ended, I managed to get Scott out of that Hell hole and went to the only place I could
think of. "Kayla, I need your help. I'm downstairs, but stay calm when you get
down here. I'll explain everything," I said when she answered.

Less than a minute later, she was outside and helping Scott and I both out
of the vehicle. She assisted Scott up the stairs, and I managed to get my own hide up
the seventh level of Hell without any assistance. Once we were finally inside the
apartment the questions started coming fast and furious.

"What the hell happened, Will? What is going on?"

"First, he needs some water," I interrupted. She halted her interrogation
and obliged to my suggestion. "He's as high as a kite right now, so we need to help
him ride it out."

"What do you mean, 'he's as high as a kite?!' He's been clean for over a
year!" she reacted.

"Kayla, stop," I commanded. "I'll tell you everything, just give me a
chance. It's not gonna be a fun story so buckle up, but give me a chance and I'll lay
it all out for you." She nodded her head in agreement. Scott was already passed out
in the recliner. I explained the whole thing to her; Scott being voted into the Kings,
the scooter, the party, the hog tie, and my showdown with Riot.

"What did they give him?" she asked.

"I don't know. I wasn't there, and Scott is way too far gone to give me any
info. And Riot sure wasn't too forthcoming with any details," I answered.

"Well maybe you should find out!" she fired back. "This shit has to end!
You and your club are going to kill my brother!" she yelled and shoved me as we
both sat on the couch.

I firmly grabbed her wrists to get her under control. "Do *NOT* lump me in with those assholes," I seethed through gritted teeth.

"Look at your back. You *ARE* one of those assholes!" she accurately pointed out.

My voice dropped as I responded. "You might want to think about who you're talking to right now." I saw the pain, fear, and disappointment settle in her eyes. Once my brain registered my behavior, those same feelings hit me just as hard. What was this club doing to me?

"I want you to leave," she said quietly.

"Kayla, I'm sor"

"Get out!" she demanded, cutting me off. It was clear she had no interest listening to anything I had to say at this point. "I'll take care of my brother on my own and clean up your stupid club's little mess."

*****

Back at my apartment, I settled in to my laptop to whip up a quick report. I took full advantage of the situation to try to exonerate Scott.

Begin intelligence report: Following this writer's latest report, this writer was jumped by the club's Prez, Riot (real name Riot Richards), and Sergeant at Arms, Mack (real name Maclin McGillicutty), for quote "jeopardizing their enterprise." This clearly refers to the transportation and selling of illicit narcotics, the basis of the trip to Tennessee.

The club has also voted in another member, their long

standing prospect. During that celebration, the new member, Junky (real name Scott James), was strapped to a chair and force fed an unknown intravenous cocktail. In the wake of now no longer having a prospect, the club has decided to reach out to a local kid (identity unknown) that has been spotted around Griz's Garage carrying drugs. More details will be provided at a later time.

End of Report

I can't frame my beatdown as assault on an officer, because Riot and Mack would first have to know my status as a law enforcement official, but I can sure use it to spell out their knowledge of and intent to distribute narcotics. I saved the report to another flash drive, stashed it away in my vest pocket for safe keeping, then passed the eff out.

I slept for over twelve hours, and when I woke up it was approaching four in the afternoon. My body needed the rest, and I was already feeling considerably better. You know, other than all the soreness. I hit the shower and let the hot water relax my muscles for as long as it stayed warm. After getting dressed I limped out to my pickup. With as sore as my hip still was I didn't want to risk riding the bike and end up with it laying on me because my legs aren't strong enough to support the weight. I wasn't scheduled at the tavern, so I decided to make my way to Griz's Garage. It might be good for me to feel things out and get a pulse on the situation before I show up at the clubhouse again. Who better to start with than Griz, I figured.

I pulled into the lot for the garage and swung the truck into a parking spot in front of the small office area. I saw Griz standing outside with RJ. Perfect, the two guys that would give it to me straight either way and not give me any unnecessary shit about it.

"Hey slugger," Griz started as I slid out of the truck.

So much for the "no unnecessary shit" part. "Yeah, so that happened," I acknowledged.

"Listen man, I don't know what happened but that probably wasn't the best choice you could've made," RJ spoke, and I listened. "You've been a patch member, for what, a week? If that? And Junky not even a full day yet. You might want to reconsider your loyalties to the club. You know you're gonna have to answer for that stunt last night, right?"

"Yeah, I kinda figured as much." There's a lot I'm gonna have to answer to here pretty soon.

"Not a smart move, rookie," Griz chimed in.

"So what do you guys recommend?" I inquired. I genuinely needed some guidance here. I had royally screwed up in my brother's opinions and I had to step carefully to regain any sliver of respect from the club. About that time is when I noticed a kid standing in the garage, looking in our direction. "Need something?"

"Does he look familiar?" asked Griz. "Tell him to give you a big smile!" The kid approached and started mumbling something in our direction. "Speak up, boy. Open your mouth when you're talking to us!" Griz ordered before laughing to himself. That's when it clicked. My brain finally registered why this kid seemed familiar. This was the teenager that Griz disfigured out behind his garage after I first got back in town. "Will, meet Jaws, our new hang-around." I could only assume the nickname came from the fact that the kid's mouth was still wired shut.

"Man, these nicknames," I thought to myself. I mean, am I right? I slowly nodded my head and stuck out my hand. The kid's handshake was like a limp fish. "Come on, act like you mean it," I advised him. "Your handshake is your first impression. You don't want people walking away thinking you're some kind of candyass, do you?"

"Will, the kid needs some menial work to earn a little cash. Think you could talk to the tavern about him bussing some tables or washing some dishes or something?" Griz asked.

"What, is he not qualified for your fine, upstanding business?" I asked sarcastically. "I'll see what I can do," I conceded.

"Go away kid, we're talking here," RJ interjected. "Will, you might wanna create some space between you and the club for a little while. Let Riot cool off so he doesn't overreact and do something foolish. I'll see if I can talk him down a little."

"Thanks RJ, I appreciate it. That's exactly what I needed to know." I appreciated his candor, even if it meant taking a step back and putting my investigation on hold for now. I had to be smart and not risk the whole mission. I left the garage and made a fast stop at the Gas N' Go bathroom to make my drop.

I scouted the landscape as I pulled up to the side of the building and didn't see anything alarming, so I hobbled over to the bathroom door and tossed my package in the trashcan on the way inside. I really hope the DEA had this figured out and were getting my intel.

Chapter 23

The next few days passed quietly enough. I stuck to my shifts at the tavern and spent some quality time with myself at my apartment when I wasn't working. Kayla hadn't shown much interest in talking to me since the ordeal with Scott and the instance between her and I that followed. Luckily I've gotten good at being alone in my lifetime; even if it's been nice to have some company lately, it's not like I've forgotten how to carry on. This too shall pass, right? Isn't that what they say? The bright side is my body had plenty of time to recoup.

Sunday night finally rolled around and I knew I was due at the clubhouse for church. This was my first appearance since Scott's party. I rolled into the clubhouse, quietly made my way to the meeting room and grabbed a seat with as little fanfare as possible. The last thing I wanted to do was rub my presence in anybody's face right now.

Once everybody had filed in and taken a seat, Riot called the meeting to order. From my chair in the far back corner of the room, I could plainly see the faint green remnants of the shiner I gave him several days ago. "Alright, there's some issues that need addressed so let's get to it. First order of business: Griz, any news on the hang-around front?"

Griz nodded his head and spoke up, "Yeah. I tracked him down and talked to him the day after the last meeting. He seemed into it, so I've had him hanging around my garage a little bit to acquaint myself with him more. I asked Legacy about getting him on at the tavern so we can keep an eye on him." I could hear the steam spewing from Riot's ears at the mention of my nickname.

The room fell quiet for a minute, so I took the lead and spoke up. "I talked to the owner the other day about getting the kid a few shifts a week. He just needs to stop by so the owner can meet him." I shut it down with that, trying to give the information I had but not wanting to drone on needlessly.

Riot appeared to completely ignore my contribution and continued to address Griz. "This is your baby Griz. If it doesn't work then cut the kid loose. Otherwise, any issues will be your issues."

"Got it, Prez," Griz acknowledged.

"Onto topic #2. Mack, you wanted to address the room?"

"Everybody here knows what happened this week," he started. His gaze bore right through me. "We can't have any member of this club taking swings at our Prez, let alone some asshole that's been in the club a matter of days." The sound of crickets filled the room. There was so much awkward tension, nobody knew how to react. "I propose another vote. I move that Legacy's patch be stripped and he be voted out of the Kings!"

"Now wait a damn minute!" I spoke up. The room buzzed now with people whispering in all directions. "*Does* everybody know *exactly* what happened this week?! 'Cuz I'm willing to bet not." I took a second to let my statement settle across the room. I could see a slight panic in Riot's eyes while Mack just met my glare with his own icy stare. The whispering ceased as everybody looked at me in confusion.

"Are you talking about how you got butt-hurt because Junky relapsed?" Riot tried to bend the truth and the club to his will.

"Relapsed?! Are you shitting me??" I fired back. "I'd say it's hard to relapse when you have both arms strapped to a chair! You know exactly what you did."

"I have no idea what you're talking about," Riot feigned innocence. "Mack and I simply got the boy a lap dance from one of our admirers. Whatever happened back there after that is between the two of them. Junky, do you have any recollection of the events?"

"Man, I barely remember her tying me down. Everything after that is a fog," Junky offered. Great, I'm screwed.

"I've thought about this long and hard. We've heard Mack's thoughts and heard Junky's input. This isn't something I take lightly, but it's something the club needs to address. We'll go around the room, one-by-one, majority decision. As the Prez, I'll start with my vote, then Mack will go next since it was his proposal. Out."

Mack's stare down hadn't drifted from me yet, so why would it now. "Out," he voted.

Following those two, you could feel the weight of the topic, as each member slowly placed their votes, some with explanation. "He's been cool to me, so in," said Stitch.

A couple guys later, El Capitán placed his vote. "Legacy, I don't know enough about you so I gotta stick with my Prez. Sorry. Out."

Scott kept it simple. "In."

Slowly, the votes added up. The brothers that were familiar with me gave a favorable vote, leaning heavily on my unofficial history with them and the club. Unfortunately, there were just as many of Riot's guys that didn't have any sentimental connection with me. After going completely around the room, it came down to one last vote which would be the determining factor. I know, who saw that coming? I breathed a sigh of relief, knowing that the VP would have my back.

RJ took his sweet time, rubbing his temples with his hands. He opened his mouth to speak and his voice caught. He stared down at the table to avoid eye contact with everyone. "Sorry kid, you went too far. Out."

Wait, what?! What in the blue Hell just happened?? I stared off into space, totally stunned. Speaking of who saw *that* coming! I was unsure of what to do or say, so I just sat there motionless.

Riot spoke up, "Will, we're gonna need that patch back." You could hear the joy in his voice, no matter how much he tried to cover it up.

I stood up, and you could see every single member in the room tense up. A "bad out" as it's called, never goes down smoothly. A biker never willingly gives up his colors, and the Kings knew this wasn't going to be pretty. On the contrary, I had already taken too many beatings for this club and from this club to be bothered enough to give a shit anymore. I slid my vest off and for a very brief second considered throwing it on the floor, but as I already said, it's not worth the hassle. So I tossed it on the table, and shook my head as I walked out of the room. My head hung so low, it was almost level with my slumped shoulders. Now what? How in the Hell was I supposed to continue my investigation following this?

Chapter 24

In the days that followed, I found myself wandering around town like a lost little puppy. My whole purpose for returning to Rough River Falls had gone down the drain. On top of that, Kayla hadn't really seemed too interested in messing with me anymore either. I guess that was probably for the best. The last thing she needed in her life was me and my disaster of a secret mission.

I kept up my shifts at Rusty's because I simply didn't know what else to do. The DEA was in a holding pattern as far as I knew. I told them about what had transpired, but pleaded my case for more time. I had no idea how to do it, but I refused to fail. The closest I could get to the club was sharing a shift with Jaws a couple times a week. Scott would stop in from time to time, but if any of the other members were around, then he wasn't free to speak to me. Even Griz and RJ, when they came in for food or a drink would grab a table instead of sitting at the bar to make sure they could rely on a waitress and avoid me. This was probably the first time in history that a bartender was the loneliest person in the building. That went on for the better part of a month, until one random night I finally got a break.

"Hey," Kayla said reluctantly.

"What do you need?" I asked, grabbing a couple glasses from behind the bar. Our interactions had been strictly business related since the night Scott was voted into the Kings.

"I need to talk," she opened up. Her gaze softened and I could actually see the color of her eyes instead of the frost that she had been throwing my way for the past few weeks. "After work, if you don't have anything else going on, I'd like you to come up to my place for a little bit."

"Umm, yeah. Sure." I worked hard to contain my excitement and be as casual as I could. The night was nearly over, but what little time remained in the shift took its sweet time to pass by. I would catch Kayla looking in my direction from time to time, confirming that she might be coming back around to me. She would avert her gaze as soon as I spotted her though, so it's not like she was openly reaching out to me.

Eventually, last call passed and we were able to get everything shut down and cleaned up before I followed her upstairs to her apartment. I sat on the couch and she occupied the recliner. It was clear she was unsure how to proceed. Before she could begin, there was a knock on the door. My heart rate picked up, unsure of what was going on. "Come in," she called from her seat. The door opened and Scott strolled in.

"What's up man?" I asked and nodded in his direction. "Is this some kind of intervention or something?" I attempted to break the ice and lighten the mood.

Kayla broke a smile. "Something like that. Will, Scott told me what's happened. He's assured me that you did everything you could to help him, and apparently all you've gotten out of it is kicked out of the club and deserted by me. I was mad as hell when you brought him here that night. All I knew was that he'd fought tooth and nail to clean himself up and stay that way, then you come into town, get voted in to the Kings, and less than a week later Scott gets voted in and you drag him here doped out of his mind. Hell yeah I was pissed."

Curious to see where this was going, I just listened.

"Scott has tried to explain to me that you had nothing to do with it and that you aren't the same as those other assholes. I guess I wasn't ready to hear it until now, especially with the way you handled me that night. So I wanted to get together and see what your side of the story is."

I could see Scott bristle at the mention of me being physical with his sister. She must not have shared that with him until now.

"I get it. I broke your trust. Don't worry Scott, I didn't do anything to hurt her, I just used a little more muscle than was necessary." Wait, what the Hell does that even mean? Was I trying to minimize the fact I had put my hands on Kayla? "But I assure both of you, my need for the club is different than those other ass-clowns." I could see I had intrigued both of them. Crap, I really needed to tread lightly here and not give away my true purpose. "Look, I have a long, messed up history with this club. I wanted to confront that history face-to-face, and come out the other side. It didn't quite go down that way. That history stared me down, chewed me up, and spit me back out, only reminding me that I wasn't made for that world." Screw it, time to put it all on the table. "I wasn't made for that world, because I was made for the opposite world." I could see their ears perk up. "When I left the Air Force, I was contacted by the DEA. I'm here to look into the Olsen incident and I jumped at the chance to bring down the Kings."

I could tell that I had just verbally assaulted both Kayla and Scott as the air was completely sucked out of the room. Nobody spoke for several minutes.

"Well now there's a whole lot more to talk about, but for the time being let's focus on what has already transpired," Kayla started. "I just don't want Scott to end up like Brad," she commented. I scrunched up my face out of confusion about who the hell Brad was. She must've caught on. "Brad Olsen. The Representative's son." Umm, what were they telling me and why hadn't this come up sooner? "Scott knew Brad. His death is what served as the wake-up call Scott so desperately needed."

"So you were friends with the Olsen kid?" I asked Scott, trying to keep my head from exploding.

"I wouldn't say we were friends," he answered. "His family owns a pretty good-sized farm past the state park, so we were familiar with each other. He was well aware that I had connections and he had no issues taking full advantage of those connections."

My thoughts were swimming so bad I couldn't think straight. And by "swimming," I mean "desperately trying to doggy paddle so they didn't drown." After learning this handy piece of business, I just sat back as much as possible and let Scott and Kayla do the talking. I would prod when necessary to clarify some details or dig up some more info, but for the most part I just let them guide the conversation. That was exactly what I needed to get back on track and possibly start wrapping things up with this investigation.

To say I slept much that night after I left Kayla's apartment would be lying. I was just handed the most useful intel against the Kings I'd been able to gather since I arrived back in town, but to use it would directly incriminate Scott since he was the provider for the Olsen boy. I also now had to worry about my secret getting out since I spilled the beans. Things just got a lot more complicated.

Chapter 25

Over the course of the next several days, I mulled over exactly how to present my recent findings to the DEA. The Agency was already well aware of Scott's lowly stature with the club, so I needed to use that to my advantage. I knew I couldn't sweep this under the rug, since it directly related to the sole purpose of my investigation, but I also knew that I had to keep Scott out of it. For Kayla. For himself. For me. The rest of those bastards could fry.

I floated around the next few days, aimlessly going from my apartment to the tavern and Kayla's. She thankfully started to thaw toward my presence since there were no more secrets, and I was more than happy to have the company. Plus, it was helpful to see if I could glean any more information from her or Scott. How many times has a woman ever complained that she's just being used for her brain? Well, I wasn't using her *completely* for her brain, but I digress.

Scott had really loosened up around me since my arrival in town, but now it was only in the privacy of his sister's apartment. He still had to keep appearances with the club that he was icing me out, just like the rest of the brothers had been doing. Let's be real though, in Smallville, USA there are no secrets, so it's not like the guys weren't aware of my involvement with Kayla, I think they just overlooked it because they had such a low opinion of Scott.

As we all sat around Kayla's apartment one night after work, I couldn't help but get a little curious. "How's the new hang-around fitting in?" I asked. I knew I was pushing my luck asking such a direct question about club business, but I felt pretty confident and safe that Scott wasn't too cautious of me. After all, less than a month prior I was a full part of the club. Plus I had nothing left to hide from him at that point.

"Eh, he's alright, I guess. You can tell he doesn't really fit in with the MC world, but Griz is trying his damnedest to get him acclimated. I'm not sure he's totally into it. I kind of have a feeling that he's just in it for the same reasons I got into it, before he and I ever started hanging out."

He's using buddies with Jaws too?? Dammit Scott, quit holding out on me! And quit putting yourself right in the middle of everything!

"He had the opposite reaction than me when Brad died," Scott continued. "Instead of getting clean, Jaws dove in even deeper. He started stalking club members that had access to things. He even found out where the Kings's stash house is, and started breaking in and stealing drugs so he didn't have to buy them."

Holy shit, this conversation just got real. Like really real. And I may have just come up with my way out for Scott. "Stash house?" I asked, wanting more information but trying to keep as quiet as possible to keep Scott talking. And I let him keep talking as much as he wanted.

"Yeah, you know, where they keep their supply," he went on.

"Yes, Scott. I know what a stash house is," I condescended. "I just didn't know what the Kings had going on." This is where I had to tread very lightly. If I got too pushy, Scott could shut down on me and leave me in the dark. "I mean, I guess the backpacks have to come from somewhere," I acknowledged, hoping Scott would tell me exactly where they came from.

"Yep, they sure do." He didn't expand any further than that, but he didn't stop talking altogether at least. "Once the Kings found out they were missing some product they set up some surveillance, and that's when Jaws started getting some beatings on the regular. He was usually pretty good at evading the Kings, but every once in a while he'd be too strung out and would do something stupid. That's when the guys would get their hands on him."

Like jump the fence by Griz's Garage. I was all too familiar with what happened when the club caught up to him. "So who runs the stash house? Wouldn't they be in some danger from the Kings for not covering the club's business??

"I'm sure the club wasn't amused, but it's not like they're just gonna start rat-packing other Kings." I threw him a deadpan look, clearly not entertaining the idea of "loyalty" when it comes to battering other members. "Oh, right," he conceded. "Well, I highly doubt they'd beat down other officers."

Ding, ding, ding. We have a winner, folks! Without saying anything, Scott had just told me everything. This investigation was about to shift into overdrive. I tried my best to hide my excitement about what I'd just heard, but I'm sure Scott and Kayla were aware of my sudden mental departure. I feigned a couple yawns, then excused myself so I could get back to my apartment. I had some thinking to do, and distractions would not be helpful. Plus I kinda needed a little privacy, you know, since nobody in Rough River Falls knew what I was up to aside from Scott and Kayla.

*****

In the solitude of my apartment I could start piecing everything together. I had some direction on where to start looking. And the best part: I now had a way to keep Scott from getting wrapped up with the aftermath.

I grabbed a notebook and started jotting down notes haphazardly, considering all of the possibilities of who was in charge of the stash house and where it's located. Griz isn't an officer, so him and the garage were out. Riot wouldn't put himself in that much of a risky position, and there's no way he'd be willing to sacrifice Mack either. That left RJ and El Capitán. And then it all hit me; the club's infatuation with the library and El C's wife being the sole librarian in the tiny town. That's gotta be where they kept their supply.

That night, decked out in all black, I decided to do a little recon around the library. I drove my truck so I wouldn't alert anybody with the exhaust note from my bike, and to keep nosy neighbors from spotting me lurking in the shadows, donning my Johnny Cash getup. I kept my distance, parking down the block on one of the side streets where there weren't any streetlights.

It would be awesome for me to tell you about the night-vision goggles and thermal imaging equipment and all kinds of other fun surveillance gear that I was issued by the DEA just for this scenario, but that would be a lie. I had to keep it really simple and low key just in case somebody happened to wander up on me. It would be hard enough to explain why I was scoping out the library in the dead of night with a pair of binoculars, let alone if I had thousands of dollars of high-tech equipment in my lap.

It didn't take long at all, and I had already started to get a feel for the amped up surveillance around the town's library. I'd never noticed it before, but now that I was actively looking for it, it really stood out. I mean, we're talking about a modest library in the middle of nowhere here, and there was a surveillance system like it's the damned Library of Congress!

I used the illumination of my cell phone to draw a rudimentary map of the library in my notebook, labeled all of the cameras I could locate, then I repositioned and continued labeling.

I was just about to wrap it up and call it a night, when I spotted an old beat up Buick pull up behind me. Three guys climbed out, and approached my truck. My heart jumped into my throat as I plummeted down into the seat to try and hide my presence in the vehicle. I could hear the voices as they approached. All I could do was sweat bullets and pop my knuckles. Had Scott sold me out?! The volume of the voices hit a peak before starting to fade again as the guys reached my truck and continued walking toward the back of the library. I waited a minute to make sure they had safely passed by, then I peeked my head just to the top of the dashboard so I could see out the windshield. I easily made out the silhouettes of Griz, RJ, and El C as they descended a few steps to the back door of the library. I reached up and unscrewed the dome light in the roof of the pickup so that I could open the door without being called out by my own vehicle.

I followed the steps of the three Kings and tracked their movement, checking the door for more security features like finger print scanners or things of the sort. I had to be careful to keep my face hidden from the security cameras that were pointed in my direction too. Not only did I not see anything beyond a good, old fashioned padlock on the door, but I instantly discovered they had left it unlocked when they went in. What a bunch of masterminds I was dealing with here. I leaned toward the crack in the door to see if I could hear anything on the other side. After listening intently for several moments, I was satisfied that there was minimal risk in trying to sneak a peek inside. I cautiously craned my neck around the side of the door and saw nothing alarming, so I slowly pulled the door open and slid inside.

I stepped into a mostly bare storage room with a couple of unused bookshelves and a rack of cleaning supplies. On the back wall I noticed another door that was wide open, and inside the other room were three big, bad bikers. I quickly and quietly removed myself from their sightlines and ducked behind one of the empty bookcases. My training kicked in out of instinct and I gathered as much information about the situation and my surroundings as I possibly could, in what I felt to be a safe amount of time. Before I overstayed my welcome, I silently padded back to the exterior door of the storage room and stepped outside as I heard the three brothers approaching. Shit, there's no way I could get to my truck without being spotted. I kept my head down so the cameras couldn't tattle on me, and I ran to the side of the building where I could use some bushes to hide. I knelt in the shrubbery and watched the Kings waltz back to the Buick without a care in the world. They had no clue that I had just discovered their homemade chemistry lab and storage facility in the basement of the library. So much for El C being the most "normal" member of the MC. No wonder they dedicated so much of their time and effort toward that building. Anytime there's been any weather damage or vandalism done to the little book depository, the club is always the first there to lend a helping hand.

Chapter 26

Begin intelligence report: Since arriving in Rough River Falls, this writer has been successful at infiltrating the Kings of Chaos Motorcycle Club. This organization is believed to be responsible for being the source of illicit narcotics related to the overdose of Representative Olsen's son, Brad.

In my time with the club, this writer bore witness to multiple felony offenses. This writer was present when long-time member Grizzly (real name Lester Peters) battered a local teenager for trespassing, resulting in the young man's face being disfigured. That individual would later become the newest Hang-Around, Jaws (real name Chad Barkley). This writer was introduced to the use of cocaine by full patch member, Stitch (real name unknown). This writer witnessed the exploitation and extortion of local businesses. This writer also has first-hand knowledge of the transportation of drugs across state lines, and was present during a shootout that likely ended in a homicide. On more than one occasion, this writer was personally the victim of being assaulted by the President, Riot (real name Riot Richards), and Sergeant at Arms, Mack (real name Maclin McGillicutty). Attached you will find images of the injuries this writer sustained from those beatings. This writer also discovered the forced use of illicit narcotics on full patch member Junky (real name Scott James) by the President, Riot, and Sergeant at Arms, Mack.

Through my investigation, this writer discovered that the Kings of Chaos Motorcycle Club used the basement area of the local library for storage and the preparation of illicit narcotics for distribution. The Kings of Chaos Motorcycle Club likely gained access to this facility through the Road Captain, El Capitán (real name Nick Fuller), due to his wife being the sole librarian in Rough River Falls. The wife's knowledge of the presence of the narcotics is unknown.

By the use of a criminal informant, the long-time Prospect, Junky, this writer was advised that the Kings of Chaos Motorcycle Club was directly involved in the distribution of illicit narcotics directly to Brad Olsen, the use of which ultimately resulted in his death.

During the course of this investigation, this writer gained first-hand knowledge of all of these offenses with the aid of a single criminal informant, full patch member Junky. This writer respectfully requests that any offenses committed by this individual be forgiven and dismissed based on his willingness to assist in this investigation.

I swear under the penalty of perjury for all of these things to be presented as truth.

Signed,

Special Agent Will McGee

End of Report

Begin operations report: Given the previous intelligence report, this writer is completely satisfied with the level of intelligence gathered and believes this investigation to have reached its conclusion. The Kings of Chaos Motorcycle Club has committed multiple felony offenses on an organized level, demonstrating the corruption of the entire organization, and this writer has connected the distribution of illicit narcotics directly to the contribution to the premature death of Brad Olsen.

At this time, it is requested that this writer be removed from the area of Rough River Falls, KY prior to the apprehension of the above named individuals. Arrests would most efficiently be made on a Sunday evening, while the Kings of Chaos Motorcycle Club would be conducting an official weekly meeting. All full patch members are required to be in attendance, making the end result of this operation go as smoothly as possible.

End of Report

Now that I had that out of the way, I needed to get that info to the DEA ASAP. With any luck, I could be out of this town by the end of the week and this nightmare could finally come to an end. Considering all that had happened, I couldn't help but feel a little like I was betraying my roots. A lot of those guys had known me my entire life. Rough River Falls is where I'm from, and I was days away from ripping out its identity. On top of all of that, I was playing a heartless game with two people that I had come to care for. Kayla and Scott didn't deserve this. They didn't ask to be sucked into my black hole of an existence. The only thing they have known for their entire adult lives is suffering, and I had only been adding to it.

I'm not too sure I could possibly hate myself much more than I did at that moment. I just had to keep reminding myself, by squashing the Kings I could exact a little revenge for my adolescent self, and hopefully keep other people from having to go through anything similar...namely the young neighbor at my apartment building. I had to do this for him. I couldn't stand the thought of him growing up the way I did – without anybody that gave a shit about him because they were too busy playing Rebel Without a Cause. But what consequence would there be after this sting went down? Once those guys were all locked up, there would be a permanent absence in that kid's life and not just a figurative one.

Was this all a giant mistake? This town and club had coincided for this long, maybe I'm out of line. Maybe Rough River Falls needs this club. There certainly isn't anything else this place has to offer. I had to stop thinking about it. "Those guys are criminals," I said to myself out loud. "They made the choice to live outside the law, now it's time to pay up for those decisions. This town will be better off for it...eventually."

Fatigue was setting in. I'd been going pretty much non-stop since two nights ago at Kayla's when I started putting all the puzzle pieces together, and my tank was hitting empty. I needed to make this drop, then I could go back to my apartment, rest up, and wait to see the fruits of my labor.

I went out to my truck with the bright morning sun drilling my brain straight through my eye holes. I hope that sounded as unpleasant as it felt. I grabbed some sunglasses from the visor in my pickup and threw them on my face before cranking on the ignition. The truck fired up and I sat there for a few minutes, observing the scene before me.

The neighbor boy was outside, running around again with no supervision. I couldn't stop myself from thinking back to when I was about ten years old. I dug up a couple dusty old baseball gloves from a closet at home. I took one to my dad who was sleeping on the couch to see if he wanted to play some catch, only I couldn't get him to wake up. After shaking him and forcing his eyes open with my fingers, there were still no signs of life. I ran next door to my grandparent's house, and eventually an ambulance was called. That was the first time I witnessed my dad overdose, but it wouldn't be the last. I shook the memory from my head and drove downtown toward the Gas N' Go.

I pulled up alongside the building where the outdoor restrooms and my personal mailbox delivery system posing as a trashcan were. I dropped my package in the receptacle, then turned back to my truck when my eyes locked on the library sitting on the corner across the street. Man, right in the middle of town. Let me tell you, what the Kings lacked in brains, they made up for in cojones. I'm talking big ol' massive balls. The kind of grown-man balls that any guy would be proud of. Alright, I hope you get the picture. Frankly, I'm tired of talking about balls. I closed my eyes and shook my head as I let the feeling of shock melt from my brain as the reality set in. Why would I even be shocked anymore? I meandered back to my apartment like I was on a Sunday drive without a care in the world, suddenly feeling a weight lifted from my shoulders. Now that the work was done, it was time to sit back and wait.

Chapter 27

A couple days later, I awoke with a start. There was an unfamiliar male standing over me in my bedroom. My heart stopped. My brain threw scattered thoughts out every millisecond. Did the Kings find out about me? Was this how it all ends? My body produced so much nervous sweat that I had to consider the idea that I had just pissed all over myself. Hell, maybe I did. All I could make out was a black silhouette, showered in darkness. But it wasn't hard to decipher that this dude was big. From the backlighting, I could make out the outline of his hands and I didn't spot any weapons, so at least I had that going for me. I abruptly barrel-rolled to the far side of the bed to avoid any coming onslaught from the stranger. Still, he stood stoically. Mesmerized by my cat-like reflexes no doubt.

"McGee, it's time to go," he stated cryptically.

"And where exactly are we going?" I questioned.

"Out of town."

This guy had some serious skills when it came to talking without actually saying anything. I could tell by his lack of a southern drawl that he wasn't from around here. Luckily for me, my training hadn't abandoned me like my parents had, and I could still pick up on little details to aid in reading a situation. I began to let myself relax, feeling pretty confident I knew what was happening. "Do I need to pack?"

"If you want to change clothes at some point, then yeah, you should pack. Make it quick though. I have to get out of here before people start stirring and notice me here. I'll take your bags with me, then you can follow me on your bike if you want." So this was my handler from the DEA that I was never formally introduced to.

"This is happening then, huh? Where am I going?" My question still stood.

"You'll be put up in Owensboro until the smoke has blown over. It's big enough of a city that nobody will know you're there, but not big enough that people will think to look for you there…the definition of anonymity. This apartment will remain in your name and the rent will be kept up, so don't worry about all of your stuff, but you will want to grab the necessities."

I quickly ransacked my apartment, grabbing toiletries and throwing them into a duffle bag along with some clothes. I managed to stuff the duffle bag and a backpack in the span of 15 minutes, then it was time to split. I stepped out of my apartment, looking back over my left shoulder to the apartment next door. The front door was open and I could see the neighbor boy standing behind the screen door. My heart shattered for him, knowing how hard his life was going to be. I shook my head and followed the agent to his blacked out SUV. "Yeah, real subtle," I thought to myself. You know, anonymity and whatnot.

"We'll take 54 the whole way in," was his only instruction.

"Let me gas up before we leave town. I'd rather not have to stop."

We mounted up separately and drove downtown toward the Gas N' Go. I peeled off from the two vehicle caravan and pulled up to the gas pumps. My handler kept driving out of town where he would stop down the road and wait for me to meet up with him. The last thing we couldn't have happen was to tip our hands and blow the whole thing, and if anybody saw me with a blacked out SUV driven by a guy in a standard issue government agent suit then you can bet the whole thing would be blown.

I topped off my gas tank and went inside to pay. On the way back to my bike I saw Scott whiz by on his scooter. I couldn't help but giggle to myself a little bit. Then I realized the direction he was headed and panic sank in. He was driving in the direction of Clubhouse Road. I had to get to him and stop him. I wasn't sure when the bust was going to occur, but I couldn't let him be there when it happened. I jogged the last few steps to my bike, threw my leg over the saddle, hit the ignition, and spun out of the gas station to try and catch up.

By the time I turned onto Clubhouse Road, Scott had already parked his scooter and was walking into the clubhouse. I revved my bike and honked my horn to get his attention and keep him from going inside. There was no way I would be welcome inside, so I had to keep him from going in. Luckily, I got his attention. He turned to see what the commotion was, then raised his hand to wave once he recognized me. Apparently, all of the noise had garnered some unwanted attention from inside the clubhouse as well.

As I got closer to the club's property, a gunshot rang out. The startling sound rattled me, causing me to dump the bike in front of a dumpster on the corner of the clubhouse's lot. My bike continued to slide beyond the cover of the metal container, but I was lucky enough to keep myself from being exposed. I peeked my head out around the corner of the large trash bin, and was met with another report in my direction. This one ricocheted off the pavement a few feet between me and my bike. I instinctively pulled back behind the dumpster, but not before I had spotted Scott running and ducking for cover. "GET OUTTA THERE, SCOTT!" I yelled from behind my cover.

"Better get comfortable back there, you prick!" came the grizzled shout from inside the clubhouse, followed by yet another potshot meant to keep my attention and show that there was no turning back.

"Hey asshole! You've made your dad reeeeeal proud!" came another shout from the clubhouse, each word dripping with sarcasm. Just to confirm my suspicion that nobody was proud of me, a bullet whizzed by my head and hit the gas tank of my bike. Fortunately, I had at least a little luck on my side as my bike didn't immediately burst into a giant fireball. "Why don't you step on out here and get dead real quick?"

"Hey! Take it easy on my bike! What did it ever do to you??" I yelled back. They don't own sarcasm.

There, so now we're all up to speed. Seriously though, how in the blue Hell did they figure out what was going on? I replayed the last several months back in my head to see where I might've slipped up, and nothing jumped out at me. Had Scott run his mouth? Some might not imagine this would be the best time to rethink everything, but what else am I gonna do? Step on out and get dead real quick, as was so eloquently offered? I think I'd rather not do that.

I moved straight back from the dumpster, keeping it between me and the clubhouse, to try and see what Scott's situation was. I noticed him behind a tree on the other side of the property, cowering in a kneeling fetal position, similar to what you'd see in the hallway of an elementary school during a tornado drill.

"SCOTT!" I yelled. His head slowly rose as he craned his neck to look in my direction. "Is all this from you?" I asked. He shook his head vigorously, his eyes as wide as the wheels on his scooter. "Get outta here!" I implored him again. I didn't want him on the scene of a shootout involving an undercover DEA agent and the MC that he's a full patch member of. Although, on second thought, if local police pulled up right now, they would have to notice that Scott is in just as a precarious position as me. They would have to recognize and acknowledge that, right? Maybe I'm giving Andy and Barney too much credit. Police work in this area doesn't really draw the most qualified candidates, as you could probably imagine.

"Maybe you should worry more about yourself, right now!" came another shout from the clubhouse.

I crept toward the far end of the dumpster to try and sneak a peek from a different vantage point. Hopefully I could get a look without drawing attention. Fortunately, I was able to quickly survey the scene before pulling my head back to the safety of my cover. Unfortunately, however, the scene just got a lot scarier. The front door of the clubhouse was now wide open, and I counted three Kings exiting the structure, minimum.

"Get the hell outta the way, Junky," I could hear Mack order. "Worthless addict," he continued mumbling.

I nervously popped my knuckles. Sweat ran from my forehead into my eyes. More sweat ran from my back into my ass crack. Yeah, gross, I know. I wasn't sure what to do here. I wasn't packing as I had loaded my weapon into my luggage, expecting to be booking down the road at this point. "Just stay alive," I said to myself. I'm sure somebody had to have heard the gunshots. Backup is on the way, it has to be!

"Where are all the smartass wisecracks now?" Mack heckled me. "Better get them out while you can."

He was right, it was now or never, only I couldn't think of a single thing to say. If I'm being completely honest with you, I was clueless here. I was pinned down with nowhere to run and no weapon to even try to defend myself.

CLANG! The sound jolted me back to reality. From the proximity of the noise, I could tell at least one of the guys was directly around the corner of the dumpster from where I currently sat. Instinctively, I reached down and grasped the largest rock I could find. It wasn't much, but it was gonna have to work. I backhanded the rock into the far end of the dumpster from where I was, praying that the diversion would avert their attention, even for a second. Without giving it anymore thought, I sprung from my position and met the backside of Griz. My trick worked, and I was able to get the drop on the stereotypical, gun-toting biker.

I raised both arms above my head, locking my hands together, then bringing them both crashing down hard on the back of his neck. The blow instantly dropped the big guy, and his gun scuttled out of his hand by about a foot. I lunged for it, wrapping my sweat-drenched hands around the steel, before swinging it with bad intentions right into his temple. Griz crumpled to the ground unconscious.

The sound of the scuffle alerted the other two Kings to my position and they turned to see me facing them with Griz's gun pointed in their direction. We all froze for a brief moment before Mack dove toward the side of the dumpster, out of harm's way. That left RJ standing in my sights. The older biker wasn't as spry as Mack was, so there was a clear disadvantage for him.

"It doesn't have to come to this, RJ," I pleaded to the guy I'd known my entire life. Doubt crept in and started to cloud my judgement. There's no way I could possibly bring myself to fire at this man, who was around me more than my father ever was.

"Will, I wish that was the case, but it's simply not true. It does have to come to this. You know too much. You've *seen* too much. The club can't have its business getting out of our hands. I may not know exactly what you have in mind, but I do know you were snooping around the library the other night. You did a helluva job keeping your face from the camera, but it only took a matter of minutes to recognize your build and gait."

RJ jerked his arm in my direction, but before he could train his pistol on me, I squeezed the trigger on Griz's Glock. I put a round through RJ's right shoulder, sending him spinning to the ground, his gun flying out of his grip. There's no way I could shoot to kill, but I had to keep myself alive. If I die today, then this case vanishes. Sure, my report has been written and delivered, but without my testimony and cross-examination, it would get shredded in open court. This case would get tossed out and the Kings would be right back to business as usual. I can't allow that to happen. Kayla and Scott are counting on me. My neighbor boy is counting on me…even if he doesn't know it yet. No. I can't die today. I *won't* die today.

"Don't move asshole," came Mack's voice from behind me. I heard the telltale click of the hammer on his gun, as he pulled it back to cock the weapon.

Well, shit. So much for not dying today. I was so determined too! This scene was straight out of a cheesy movie. How did I not see this coming? I slowly turned to face my aggressor. "Hey Mack. Good day for a gunfight, huh?" I knew I still had it in me. There's no way my best defense mechanism could fail me now.

"Drop it," he demanded, speaking of the Glock in my right hand.

As I eased my grip on the pistol, I saw movement from behind Mack out of the corner of my eye. I presented my best poker face, not leading on to what I was witnessing. Hell, *I* wasn't even sure what I was seeing. I tossed the gun to his side, and a little beyond where he was standing. I just had to hold out a little longer.

"What's this all about?" Mack asked, uncharacteristically. For as unlucky as I've been lately, Mack's sudden interest in a conversation may just turn out to be my saving grace.

"Well Mack, I'm not sure you'd understand. This club is the sole reason for my family failing to exist the way a family is supposed to."

"Who cares? I shouldn't have asked," he admonished himself. Mack retrained his aim from my chest to my face.

"Aww, c'mon, not the face," I begged. "At least let me have an open casket for all my admirers."

That bought just enough time. Scott had quietly snuck up from behind Mack and gathered Griz's gun. He swung it fiercely, pistol-whipping Mack in the back of his cranium, dropping him like a bad habit. He stood there, staring at me in disbelief.

Behind him, I could see a blacked out SUV turn onto Clubhouse Road with red and blue lights strobing from the grill and windshield. Perfect timing. I swear, I have to be in a poorly written reality show, and everybody is in on it but me. If I hadn't been begging for my life less than sixty seconds ago, I would have to laugh about it. At this time, though, I wasn't in much of a laughing mood.

Following the shootout at the O-K Corral, I walked over to stand my bike up off the ground.

"Will, that bike doesn't look too trusty," my DEA handler quipped.

"It's fine," I replied. "If she'll start, then it'll get me where I need to be." My body was way too damn sore to even think about the kickstarter. Hell, just reaching my thumb over and hitting the electric start hurt bad enough. The ol' girl roared to life. Luck was on my side for once in my life.

"Where do you think you're going?" My handler asked.

"Away from here. Owensboro, I suppose. I'll let you handle the cleanup on this mess if you don't mind too terribly much. I'm sure there'll be some pretty serious debriefing once we finally have a chance to sit down and have a conversation, plus all the paperwork and reports to go along with the gunplay here. I have a hunch you'll find Riot, El C, and some of the other guys hanging out around the library downtown. Send them my regards." I kicked the gear lever down into first, let out on the clutch and rolled on the throttle. I made my way to Main Street and somehow managed to clear my mind. Kayla's face popped into my head and I knew I couldn't drag her down into my life any further.

I rode out of town and approached the Highway 54-110 split. As usual, I started to lean into the long sweeping curve to the right. Only this time my body wasn't strong enough to tame the bike and my mind didn't want to. My bike drifted across the left lane, onto the shoulder and into a guard rail. My body flew off the bike and I somersaulted in mid-air. Up was down, ground was sky. I couldn't keep anything straight anymore and I didn't care to even try. Finally, I felt no pain. My written report would have to be good enough. At least without cross-examination, the defense attorney won't be able to trip me up over some pointless details. One last thought entered my consciousness; Goodbye Kayla.

Extended Director's Cut Epilogue

BEEP, BEEP.

BEEP, BEEP.

I awake to the sound of a heart monitor counting out my pulse. My throat is sore as shit from being intubated. I slowly open my eyes and am flooded with bright lights. Everything is a blur for what seems like minutes, but in reality might've been twenty seconds. Once my eyes come into focus, I glance around the room. I can't move my head because of the neck brace I'm tethered to, but I still manage to spot Kayla sitting in a chair by the window. She must've sensed me looking at her because she looks in my direction for no apparent reason. She flashes a huge smile and steps over to my bedside, leaning down and kissing me on the cheek. Without speaking, she leaves the room for a split second and comes back in with Scott in tow, who's sporting his Kings cut. Now I don't know how long I've been out, but I don't see any possible way the club survived the subsequent sting that I coordinated. He approaches the bed, and I notice the patch on his chest. Prez. What the Hell?

He must've read my mind as he started talking. "I'm picking up the pieces," he acknowledged. "But this time, I'm doing it my way. The right way." He turns his back to me so I can see the colors. Noticeably absent is the diamond-shaped 1%er patch. "You get better quick, because I'm gonna need some help with this. What good is a Prez without a righteous VP?" he grins before leaving the room.

Good for you, kid. "You know, you're gonna need more than that scooter if you wanna keep wearing that "P" patch."

About the author

Charles Kelley grew up in the foothills of southern Indiana. He fled the farm lands upon graduation from high school to attend Ball State University. After receiving a B.S. in Criminal Justice/Criminology, he started his career working with various criminal justice agencies. His writing career started very modestly with a personal blog, which developed his love of creative writing, leading to his webpage of short stories. Naturally, the next step was developing bigger ideas and longer stories, AKA novels, so here we are.

He currently resides in Indianapolis, Indiana and is trying his best to raise a family, further his career, and explore his interest in writing. Any other "free time" is occupied by watching sports, riding his motorcycle, playing guitar, and traveling.

Keep up to date with news on upcoming projects by following Charles on Facebook at www.facebook.com/ckwriting. You can also check out his humble beginnings by reading some of his short stories at www.ckfiction.com.

CPSIA information can be obtained
at www.ICGtesting.com
Printed in the USA
FSHW021557160819
61099FS